IT'S HALLOWEEN

— LORE —

Again!

JOSH SPERO

Castling
Books

Castling Books

An Imprint of CASTLE BRIDGE MEDIA
Denver, Colorado

Edited by Jason Henderson & In Churl Yo
Stories by Josh Spero
Special Guest Author Leigh Fryling
Interior Art by TT Hernandez
Cover Art by Aldo Avelar

This book is a work of fiction. Names, characters, business, events, and incidents are the products of the author's imagination. Any resemblance to actual persons, living or dead or actual events is purely coincidental.

IT'S HALL-LORE-WEEN AGAIN!

ISBN: 979-8-9917855-7-0

SPECIAL THANKS

Thank you to all of you that invested in this project on Kickstarter.
Without you, this could not have been possible:

The Klein Family: Megan, Jason, Gavin, & Jaxon
Mike Grimes & Family
Andrew Nield & Family
Jason Nadin & Family
Blair Knutson

Special Thanks to K.J. Davis for your contributions
to "The Kings of Halloween".

Other Special Thanks to the Dedicated/Ride-or-Die
Hall-Lore-Ween Crew:

TT Hernandez: for vivid interiors and story chats.
Leigh Fryling: for sharpening every word & keeping me in line.
Aldo Avelar: for the eye-catching cover art & Jacko inserts.
Brett Jasper: for wrapping it in a nice shiny bow.
Bob Jasper: for designing and building everything I dream up,
no matter how far-fetched. He always finds a way to make it real.
Rebecca & Sam Estrada: Spooky Booth Crew, and partners in crime.

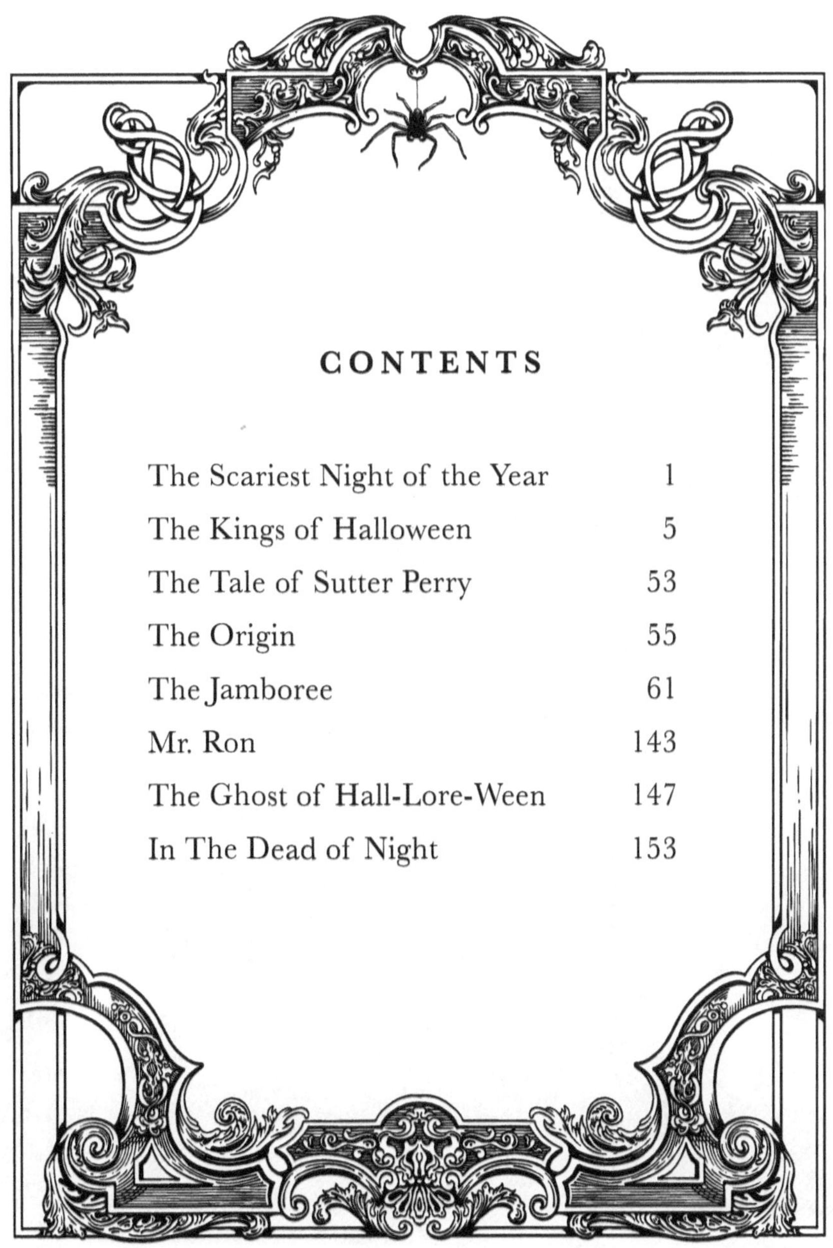

CONTENTS

Hello my frightful friends. So, the
first book didn't scare you away, huh?
Well, that's good, because I have
brought you a new batch of darkly
delicious tales that will surely make
you squirm. So, kill the light, warm
yourself under a blanket because these
stories will chill you to the bone.
Are you brave enough to dive in? Then
let the darkness unfold and the Spooky
Season commence!

But remember… You've Been Warned!

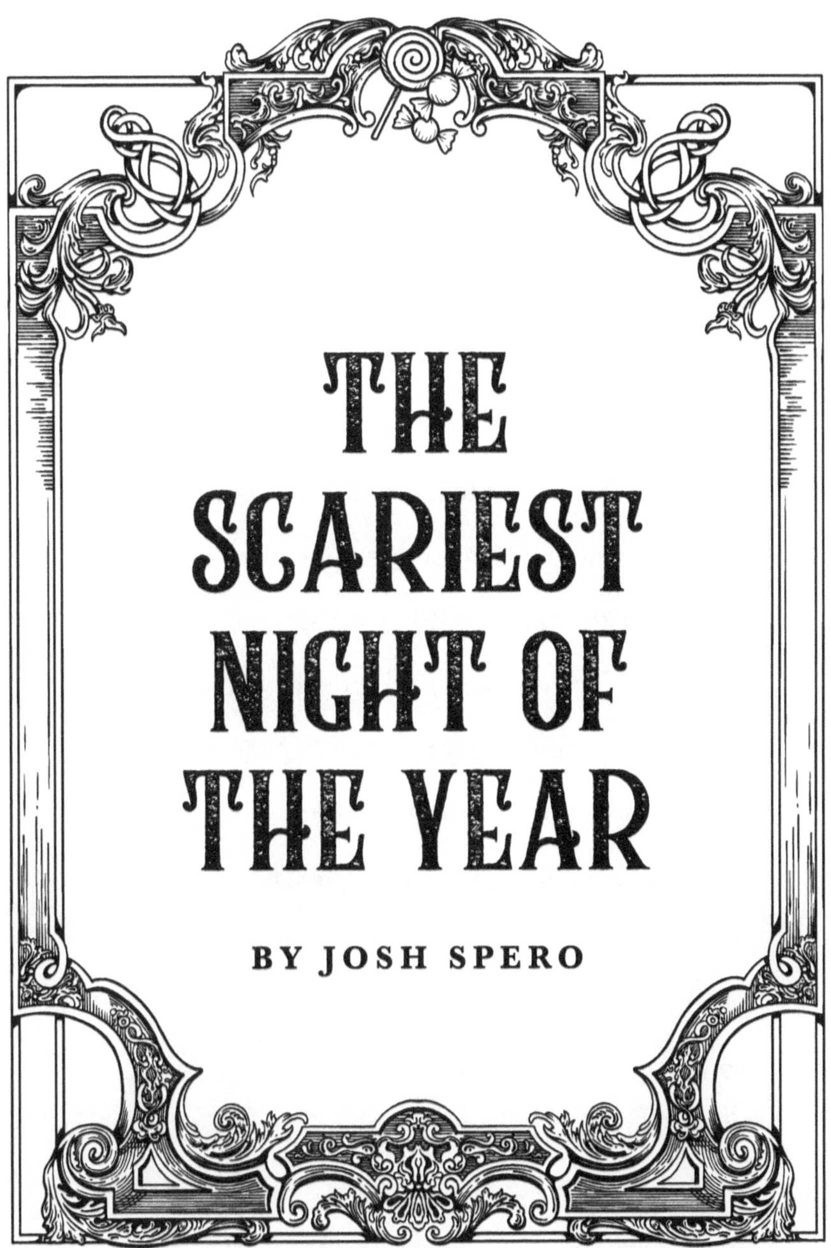

THE
SCARIEST
NIGHT OF
THE YEAR

BY JOSH SPERO

When temperatures drop and the wind starts to blow—

That's when the dead start to stir down below.

For each night that passes brings everyone near

To that ominous night that we all love and fear.

When the harvest is ready and pumpkins are ripe,

When the towns start to dress and add to the hype,

When the house's décor and the school lessons change,

To tales of the darkness so sinister strange.

The closer it creeps the more strongly you feel

The Halloween spirit grows more and more real.

For the darkest of seasons is surest to bring

The grandest affair for the Harvester King.

Select the right costume and shoes for your feet,

Meander the night shouting out "trick or treat!"

So, will you dress cutesy, or funny, or scary?

Will you scream through the streets, or will you make merry?

Is there some special book you are likely to crack,

(Like this Hall-Lore-Ween sequel you got in your sack?)

Is there a hot party for you to attend?

Or will you just hang with your best spooky friend?

Will you dare to enter the black cemetery?

Where creatures are lurking, you'd better be wary…

So here's to a new Spooky Season of fun,

There's no time to spare to get jack-o-lanterns done!

Keep the laughter and candy free-flowing all night,

And look for the ghosts in their ghoulish delight,

For Halloween's coming, it soon will be here

Let's make it the scariest night of the year!

THE KINGS OF HALLOWEEN

BY JOSH SPERO

Friday, October 18, 1974

It was a typical early morning in Akona, Minnesota and I was headed to the school library. Usually, I looked forward to the early bike ride across town because the dregs of society – I call them The Meatheads – don't arrive at any location involving "work", "learning", or "knowledge" until they absolutely have to. The early bird therefore avoids the knuckle sandwich. Unfortunately, I left later than usual because I completely overslept. No one could blame me for that, the midnight movie had been *One Million Years BC*, and I was not going to miss the double whammy of Ray Harryhausen and Raquel Welch, even if it was a school night. Consequently, the Meatheads, otherwise known as Troy, Blake, and Asher, had already spun their web. All I had to do was fly into it.

I had pedaled to this point without a care in the world as the shredding guitar riffs of Children of the Grave blared in my ears. I was just about to school when—

WHAM

My wheels locked up and I became Superman, flying over the handlebars in a single bound. The harsh caress of concrete grazed my skin through the holes in my jeans. I rolled and picked myself up, checking that everything important was still attached. Mostly minor scratches, a few fresh bloodstains, but most of the hit was taken by my self-esteem.

Troy held the long stick he'd pushed into my spokes, while the other two laughed maniacally like a pack of hyenas.

"Well, if it isn't dumbass of the year, Steven Franklin. Pay the toll, or pay the consequence, buttworm!" Troy demanded. "Lunch money, now!"

I dabbed blood from my stinging knee and sighed. I could already hear my mom swearing about my clothes. "I packed a lunch today," I said.

"Well, that don't help us much, does it, Blake?" Troy backhanded his partner's arm.

"Yeah, what's the consequence, today?" Asher blasted a snot-rocket out of his left nostril onto the leaf covered ground while blocking his right.

"He bagged his lunch," Blake wore an evil, toothy grin and wide eyes. "Make him the bag!" He smacked his own hand with a fist, inches from my face, and then pointed. "Make him wear it, Troy!"

Without delay, Troy grabbed my backpack, ripped my lunch bag out of it, and tore it wide open. The drink, chips, sandwich, and apple bounced on the ground. However, he had found his weapon of choice – my chocolate pudding. "Perfect!" he said. "Hold him down!"

Asher and Blake held me pinned in their armpits. It was hard to say who smelled worse—*deodorant* was just a vocab word on a Health class quiz to them. I heard Troy peel open the container and felt the cold thick ooze drain into the back of my pants. Why, oh why, did it have to be chocolate pudding today…

To pour salt on the wound, they tripped me, sending my feet flying out from underneath me and my back down to meet the unforgiving concrete once again. This time, it squished the brown pudding up my back, staining…well, everything. Mom wasn't going to be able to get these out.

While the Meatheads laughed, the commotion attracted the attention of other poor bastards on their way to school. There was no way they weren't looking at me. So long, self-respect. Farewell confidence. Death comes for us all.

Then, a shimmer of hope; the sun sparkled on chrome wheels, thick glasses, and deep black pens nestled in fresh pocket protectors. *My friends!* Bill and Seth to the rescue!

"Hey, Billy," pointed Seth, as their bikes skidded to a stop. "Do you smell crap or is it these cow pies in clothes?"

Billy sniffed the air. "Absolutely, a hundred percent. It's these three cow pies!"

Asher and Blake started shouting back vague obscenities, including things they would like to do to Billy's older sister Kat, and things started to look very ugly. Until Troy chimed in. "You're dead, you dweebs!" Troy yelled. He wasn't as original as his cronies, but he was louder. Too loud, this time.

"Hey!" Principal Slatman's voice boomed just in time. "No shenanigans! Get to first period, now!" He stepped toward us, and the Meatheads flinched a bit. They knew if he got close enough to see what my situation was, it would be at least a month of Saturday detention for them. Which would mean three months of extra attention on me, the last thing I wanted.

"Yeah, you heard the man, run along miscreants!" Seth said loudly, waving them off. For a moment it didn't look like Slatman was going to buy it, but a shout from a teacher pulled his attention away from us, and he left for parts unknown.

Blake snorted. "You tech dicks got lucky but watch your backs. This is not over."

Troy left for class with the other two in his shadow.

No one laughed as Billy and Seth helped me up. "Are you okay, Stevie?" Seth asked me. I did not respond. The faces of other kids as they walked past us told me everything I needed to know about how I looked, but the sympathy on their faces was just as strong. Everyone was as sick of the bullying as I was.

"I'm okay, guys. I have P.E. first period, so I'll just wear my gym clothes for the rest of the day. Nothing broken. Mostly just my pride that's hurt."

"You still have pride left this late in the year?" Billy asked. "I ran out after Labor Day."

The three of us shared a rueful grin. Seth clapped me on the back, while Billy hunted for the scattered remains of my lunch, and the three of us turned our faces toward the school building.

P.E.

Algebra

English

Chemistry

Art

Band

Shop

The day passed in a brown and orange haze of quizzes, chapters, questions and books. No one remarked on my slightly smelly gym attire. Pretty much everyone knew by lunchtime that the Meatheads had claimed another victim. Ah, well. Who was there to impress around here anyway? Nobody here but us chickens.

After school that day, the three of us pedaled back to our neighborhood. Our tires rolled over damp leaves shimmering from a recent sprinkling, and we kept our eyes peeled for loose pinecones that might send us sprawling. I let the crisp autumn breeze glide against my face and cool the hot emotions that lingered from that morning. The weekend was a marvelous realm of possibilities lying before us. Things were going to be okay.

"Hey Steven, are we still coming over for our Knights meeting?" Billy asked.

"For sure." I replied. "It's Friday. The Neutron Knights always meet on Fridays."

The Neutron Knights was the name of our science club. We always got together, watched old horror movies, and attempted a new science experiment each week. Some were pretty tame in comparison to what you saw on Mr. Wizard; we extracted the DNA from a strawberry last weekend. Not to say that it wasn't fascinating, but it didn't put much of a dent in the 'Volcano Incident'. When our baking soda and vinegar itch had been scratched, Billy suggested that we see what would happen if we put some gunpowder in a baby food jar with a long jute twine fuse for a 'real bang'. Looking back, I'm just glad we remained in one piece.

"I know. I was just checking, with all that happened this morning. That's all."

"I hate those jerks, so much," I said.

"I know!" shouted Seth. "They're going down! I have no idea how yet, but they need a taste of their own medicine."

The conversation cut short as we rode our bikes up my driveway and through the side gate, avoiding the front door and the rest of my family in favor of the back basement door. It had been decided that as the eldest and only boy I would be banished along with my teenage attitude to the basement. Joke was on them—the basement actually worked very well for me because it was a large space. Half of it was my bedroom, and the other was a homemade science lab that The Neutron Knights had collectively built over the last year and a half. We also had a sofa and a big screen setup in a separate area that we viewed the classics on. This was the headquarters for the Neutron Knights.

"Yo yo yo, guys. Let's make rainbow fire tonight." begged Seth.

"Are you kidding me?" I chimed in. "Last time we tried that, we caught Milo's tail on fire."

"He's right. His dog still has a patch where he can't grow fur." said Billy, idly replacing several loose tools back to their designated drawers. I've never been the neatest guy.

"So then, what are we thinking?" I asked.

"Exploding Pumpkins," said Billy with a grin. "Gotta stay on theme, it's spooky season."

"Hell yeah!" Seth and I agreed, our minds filling instantly with visions of orange splatter and chunks of pumpkin littering the yard.

And that's exactly what we did. We set up a station in my backyard and let the party commence.

"This is way faster than carving them," I laughed, as the mouth flew out of my second pumpkin and the triangle eyes made their way across the yard.

"What makes it do that Billy?" asked Seth, setting up the last pumpkin.

"It's when you break a chemical bond. Kinda like…you know when you snap a piece of wood across your knee, and you can feel it kinda bend and bend and bend and then SNAP! That's the explosion, the snap."

The sounds of cicadas radiated through the warm midwestern night. We were watching the last chemical reaction project small chunks of orange tissue through the air like particles of a giant unobstructed sneeze. With each explosion, we cheered and danced. My dad popped his head out of the second story window. "Steven, that's enough. Please quit while each of you boys still have all of your limbs and phalanges."

"You got it, dad!" I yelled back. "Clean up time fellas."

The sky was just starting to dip toward darkness when a small, bright purple dot appeared just below the moon. I frowned and tapped Seth on the shoulder. Stars were his thing.

"What is that, Venus?"

"What's what? That purple thing?" Seth frowned and chewed on his lip. "No. Venus doesn't move. That thing is…moving."

"What thing is moving?" asked Billy, setting the last jack-o-lantern lid in place.

"That purple…thing. Dot. Light."

The three of us watched, half in fascination, and half with a growing sense of dread as the light grew both faster and brighter. And then larger. And then all three.

"Guys…I think…"

"GET IN THE BASEMENT!" screamed Seth. "IT'S A METEOR!"

There was a mad scramble of limbs and doorframes. Thirty seconds later we were fighting for position as we stood on the back of the couch to peer through the tiny egress window.

"What's going to happen?" hissed Billy, as though whispering made you safer.

"If it hits the ground anywhere near us…say goodbye to your brains, they'll explode out your eye sockets and you'll die instantly. Human french fries, extra crispy." Seth always had a way with words.

"So…what, it's just a big explosion?" I asked, trying not to imagine shards of glass from the egress window being blown through the back of our skulls while my little sisters played Barbies upstairs in their bedroom.

"Basically. Explosion, shockwave, fire, a big hole in the ground…"

"LOOK!" Billy shrieked, right in my ear.

The thing was, we couldn't. What had been a small purple

light moving across the sky less than five minutes ago was now blisteringly bright, flashing across our retinas and leaving a red streak behind our eyelids as it passed. We all cried out, covering our eyes, and when we could see again the world was dark. We rubbed our eyes, trying to look out the window again, when a small explosive sound lit the evening air and a tiny, deep tremble shook the earth.

"Steven! I said can it!" shouted Dad from upstairs.

All three of us stopped and stared at each other in utter shock. After ten seconds of silence, and without speaking, we all started running toward our bikes.

"Wait," said Seth. "Get the hot gloves. It's going to be hot if we find it."

"Where are we going Seth?"

"The woods. Can't you smell it?"

It was weird, but he was right—there was a strange ozone smell, like the smell you get right before a thunderstorm, but there wasn't a cloud in the sky. Billy tucked the hot gloves into his belt, and I grabbed what I called my "field kit"—not much more than a kid's bug catching kit, but it did the trick for most of our basic adventures. So armed, we hopped on our bikes.

"Neutron Knights, RIDE!"

We rode for at least half an hour before we approached the edge of the woods off highway 60. Seth had a strange set to his body, like what I imagined a bloodhound 'pointing' might be—his whole body seemed tuned into a sound that neither Billy nor I could hear. Without a backward glance Seth hopped off his bike, leaned it against an oak and started marching into a wood. With a shrug and an uneasy feeling, Billy and I followed him.

We walked in silence for at least twenty minutes, before Seth started picking up his pace. The woods were getting warmer as we walked, and I took off my jacket and tied it around my waist. A thin sheen of sweat was starting to build in Billy's hair, and we could see drips of sweat in Seth's hair. Soon we discovered the source of the heat—we almost stumbled into a long thin path that smelled of smoke and ozone. The yellow and orange glow from small fires here and there lit the way.

"This is it," said Seth to the night air. "This is the path of a meteor. Come on guys, hurry up!"

We walked up the deep divot in the earth for another ten minutes. The heat continued to increase, and I worried that we would get baked or blasted with Gamma Rays or Space Waves and wind up like the Fantastic Four. My mind wandered into what kind of powers I would want to get when we finally came to a small crater, about the size of a Ford Pinto in a circle of ash blackened trees.

The heat was intense, but fading, like opening an oven. In the center of the crater was a tangle of roots and dirt and rocks.

"How are we even gonna find it?" said Billy, grimacing at the mess.

"Duh, it'll be the hottest thing in here, it'll be where the heat is coming from, follow your hands."

Seth started digging in the hole. Billy and I followed, too curious now to back out. In relatively short order we found it—Billy swore a blue streak when his hand brushed against something hot in the dark. Clenching his flashlight between his teeth, Seth checked

Billy's hand—no burn—then grabbed the hot gloves from Billy's belt.

"Ee-vee, eht eh eerie ish" he said with a mouth full of flashlight. Annoyed, Billy grabbed the light out Seth's mouth and held it up.

"Stevie, get the petri dish," he said again, eyes locked on the meteorite. I rummaged in my bag, pulling it out as fast albeit carefully as I could.

It mostly looked like a piece of what we called clunker—rock and metal bits that you could find if you walked along the railroad tracks. In that respect it was as ordinary as it could be. Where it got weird was what was inside it. The rock was split in two and glowing green ooze was leaking out of it. I scooped up as much as I could without touching it into the dish. We used the bottom and the lid sort of like plates, holding the rock and goo on them as long as we could; the glass dishes heated up quickly, and we had to put the dishes inside the hot gloves to stop our fingers getting scorched.

The ride home was much slower than the ride out. We were tired but flying high on the shock and awe of our reality. *We had a space rock.* And, subsequently, space goo.

Now what?

We stood, staring at the now cool petri dishes on the lab bench. Billy just kept shaking his head and crossing his arms.

"We need to call the police."

"What? Why?"

"We just stole a space rock my dudes! We should give it back!"

"We didn't steal anything," snapped Seth. "It fell out of the sky! We found it, it's ours."

"But," I said, secretly feeling much more aligned with Billy for once than Seth, "shouldn't we at least call NASA? I mean… this is kinda their thing. And I never read about any meteors having anything *in* them."

Seth turned to us with a light in his eyes I had never seen before. He was almost vibrating with some inner energy that I just couldn't name. Whatever it was, it scared Billy and I into silence.

"We're not calling anyone. Guys, this is OURS. Who do we read about in science class? We read about amazing scientists who *made discoveries.* Not scientists who found stuff and called the police. We need to *study this*, we need to write papers, we need to get ready to be in a science journal. We'll be the first kids ever to make this kind of breakthrough discovery…as soon as I use the bathroom. Be right back. Start prepping the microscope!"

Seth disappeared to the bathroom, and I grabbed Billy's wrist as he started to reach for the petri dishes.

"Gloves and goggles man. I don't like this. He may be right, but we are doing this safety-first all the way, no mistakes. Got it?"

"Got it."

We wasted no time setting up slides, but the revelation under the scope was disappointing. Or rather, there wasn't one. It was as though the substance from the meteorite was nothing more than green water. No crystalline structures, no living thing wriggled under the scope, just green, green, green. I grumbled to myself in frustration as Billy munched on potato chips over my shoulder.

"It's nothing, it's just water. Or something like water. I guess. I mean it doesn't have a smell, and it acts like water, but I don't feel like adding anything to it unless we're outside. Or in a real lab. I mean, I sleep down here dude."

I started prepping another slide, hoping maybe this one would have something on it.

"I hear you," said Billy. "And Seth's being a little…intense on this. What do you want to try first? pH balance test?"

He turned and stumbled a little against the bench, stubbing his toe. "Ah, crap! Ow! Sorry Stevie, I'm just so tired."

It was too late; the damage was done—my second slide now contained space goo and potato chip. I sighed.

"It's fine, just… go eat over there. Maybe it'll react to the potato chip or something."

I slid the plate under and then swore again. It wasn't a clean plate—we'd left strawberry DNA all over it from our last experiment, and like most things in the basement, it was covered in a thin layer of dog fur and probably not a little bit of dried drool—Milo was not the world's cleanest dog. The slide looked like a pink, slightly furry abstract art exhibit. I started to turn away for a new slide—and stopped cold. Something WAS moving.

"Holy moley…Billy…look!"

Under my eyes, the strawberry DNA was moving. It was… unfolding, unravelling, spreading out into the green goo. Billy pushed me aside to look, and gasped.

"STEVIE, it's… Stevie it's…nope, I don't get it, what is it doing?"

I took back over. The strawberry DNA was wiggling. That's the only word I could come up with. It was wiggling. *That*, I knew, wasn't normal.

"Look at the strawberry DNA. It's moving."

"It shouldn't do that."

"I know."

"We need to call NASA. This is too big for us. We can't see anything with this microscope."

We were silent for a moment. We loved Seth, but Billy knew I was right. This was too big for us.

"Shouldn't we wait for Seth to finish taking a crap?" Billy asked.

"Of course!" I replied. "We're sure as hell not calling NASA without him."

I reached back and pulled the plate off the microscope and put it aside carefully on the lab bench. I wondered if NASA was in the Yellow Pages.

Seth burst in.

"Torpedoes launched. The chamber's empty and so is my stomach. Oh, sweet. I love Ruffles!" Seth said as he grabbed the chip and tossed it in his mouth before we could stop him.

"NOOOOOOO!" Billy and I shouted simultaneously. Seth looked at us startled as he swallowed the chip.

"What? What? What?" he asked while panic set in.

"Dude, you just ate the space goo!" I yelled.

"What the hell! Why was it on a chip?" Seth shouted back.

"Because Billy tripped and dropped it on the slide!" I screamed. From above us, one of my parents stomped on the floor in a 'shut up or die' level of warning, and we dropped our voices to terrified whispers.

"Am I going to die?"

"I don't know Seth, which is why we should probably call NASA!"

"Absolutely, a hundred percent going to die." Billy chimed in with a nervous smile, trying to lighten the situation.

"Shut up, Billy! We don't know Seth. But the goo was doing something weird to the strawberry DNA, it was moving."

"Strawberry DNA? What are you even talking about?"

I explained as fast as I could, Billy shifting nervously from side to side next to me. Seth's face went pale, then green, then a sick but resigned sort of gray.

"If I die, I die for science," he said, solemnly.

"How do you feel though?" asked Billy, trying not to betray his own fear with a shaky voice, and instead squeaked into an upper register. I had a nasty memory of a scene from *Charlie and the Chocolate Factory* and tried not to ask Seth if he was feeling like a strawberry.

"Itchy."

"That's just your allergies," I said. "You always get itchy when you're in the basement too long."

As though on cue, my dog Milo let himself in through the dog door, collar and license jangling around his neck.

"No, not dog itchy. Itchy on the inside."

Billy snorted "what the hell does that mean?"

"I don't know, I'm trying to describe it! I'm not Socrates dude, I don't know how to describe dying!"

"YOU'RE NOT DYING," I shouted, trying to convince

myself more than anyone. "You're…changing."

Seth's eyes widened in fear. Mine must have too, because Billy's face joined ours in an expression of disbelief and horror.

"Ch-changing? How? Into what?"

Simultaneously, Billy and I turned to look at Milo, who was lying on my bed. The eye contact made Milo sit up and tilt his head garnished with an inquisitive moan. "Ha ha. Very funny." Seth said. "This is not the time for pranks you assholes."

What happened next happened without a sound. I don't know if it's because his vocal chords changed first, or if we were all just too stunned to make a noise, but nothing came out when Seth tried to scream.

Seth's fingers started to shrink. It was as though the knuckles just retreated into his joints, making what was left stumpy and exaggerated. The nails blackened and curved out as thick fur pushed its way out of the pores in his arms. His ears, like melting wax on a candle, elongated down the sides of his face before joining his arms in sprouting black and tan fur. I looked at his face, dreading what came next as his eyes sunk backwards and his nose turned leathery and black.

At this point, Milo got scared and ran out of the room with a whimper. As his knees reversed direction, Seth started screaming. He stumbled around the room bumping into things, breaking beakers and generally making a whole lot of ruckus. Amidst the chaos, we heard my dad pound the basement door.

"Is everything okay in there? I'm coming in!"

"Crap! Under the bed." I whispered to Billy. "Seth, shut up!"

They both understood, because that is exactly what we did. Immediately after he was safely tucked away, my dad flung the door open.

"What's going on in here? What is all the screaming? Is everyone okay?" My dad interrogated.

"Nothing dad. We were excited about the midnight movie, and Billy and I started roughhousing. We'll clean it up, right Bill?"

"Oh yeah. A hundred percent. Just fooling around. Sorry, Mr. Franklin."

My dad smiled.

"Not a problem, Billy. But, since I'm here, I've been meaning to check in on the famous 'Neutron Knights'."

He walked across the room and sat on the bed, which sagged under the weight of my father. We tried to keep the conversation short—yes, the exploding pumpkins were fun, yes school was good, no we didn't have homework, Seth was here, he just had to run home and get his toothbrush. Despite our best efforts, the pressure of my dad sitting on him made Seth half dog/half human head emerge from under the bed for air. Lost in conversation, my dad caught a glimpse of the furry thing.

"Oh, hey Milo! I didn't realize you were in here," he said, reaching down and petting Seth on the head.

"Dad!" I blurted out and darted up. "Ummm, I really appreciate the visit, but the movie is going to start in a little bit, and we need to clean up the mess."

"Of course, you guys do. Want some popcorn?"

"Love some, maybe later, we'll come up and make some."

"Well, I hope Seth's alright, it's dark out tonight. Very well boys. Have a goodnight." Dad said as he departed the room. The door clicked shut behind him.

"Holy crap that was close." Billy said with a sigh of relief. We both stopped and looked at Seth, who was scratching the back of his ear with his paw-like hand.

"Seth, are you okay?"

We waited eagerly. It was probably only a moment, but it felt like an hour had passed.

"Can you talk?"

Seth just stared at us for a while and then spoke. "Howwwwwww interest." He cleared his throat, something between a cough and a growl. "How interesting. I'm okay. I feel great in fact. So I'm…Milo?"

"Wow, this is far out!" Billy whooped. "You're a freaking dog, Seth! Check it out." He ran to his backpack and busted out a Polaroid camera, snapping a photo. After a few moments of shaking the picture, he showed it to him. The shock set in.

"What is going to happen to me? Am I stuck like this? What am I going to tell my Mom? Dad? What about school?" Seth's mind was reeling, and his mouth didn't hold back as he swore six ways from Sunday about missing little league tryouts because he was stuck as a basset hound lab mix in his best friend's basement.

"Alright, just calm down!" I chimed in. "We're just going to have to…watch you. Maybe it's not permanent. It never is in the movies."

"IT TOTALLY IS DID YOU NOT SEE *THE FLY?!*" Seth

was starting to panic. I don't think he really thought about it before he did it, but Billy reached up and started to pet Seth between the ears. It did the trick—Seth started to calm down.

"I know you're scared," I said. "We are too. Just… listen. Spend the night here, and let's see how you feel in the morning."

"Fine. Okay. Yeah" he said, sagging down on the couch. Billy sat to his left, still stroking him between the ears, and I sat down at his right. None of us knew what to say. Unfortunately, it didn't stay that way for long.

"Hey Seth? Don't fib about how long your wagger is. Otherwise, it'll be a tall tail. Get it? TAIL!" Billy looked way too proud of himself. I had to put him in his place.

"Hey Seth? Just remember it could be worse. Keep a paws-ative outlook." I returned. It was hard not to give in and laugh.

"Just promise that we'll all be friends fur-ever." Billy breathed, barely able to get the joke out straight.

"Yeah. If not, that would be pretty ruff, huh Seth?"

"I'd say we're having a ball right now, but I wouldn't want Seth to go chase it."

"You both suck, I hope you know that" Seth pouted, and the three of us melted into helpless, hysterical laughter. What else could we do?

Seth shook us awake at 3.

"Your dad saw me."

Billy and I both sat up straight.

"He WHAT?!"

"Saw me, I… I had to pee, and he opened the door and saw

me. Like this. But y'know…peeing."

Billy and I gaped. It was all over. We were doomed. We would be grounded until Armageddon and then some.

"Peeing like you, or peeing like a dog?"

"What?"

"You know, with one leg up."

"Billy, shut up. Seth, what did he say?"

Seth looked over his shoulder nervously. "Something about why can't he just have normal dreams about Farrah Fawcett instead of this Scooby Doo crap. Then he walked away."

Billy looked at me, torn between laughter and fear. I let out a slow breath.

"Sometimes he sleepwalks. Let's just hope it was that, okay?"

We all hunkered back down. Billy, whose superpower is the ability to sleep anywhere at any time, was out like a light. But I struggled to get back to sleep.

"Seth?"

"Yeah?"

"How are you feeling?"

A long pause.

"Dog tired."

A giggle. Then two. Then we laughed ourselves back to sleep.

When the morning came, Seth looked almost completely normal. His ears were a little distended and his hands had a little fur still on them. Billy made a joke about hairy palms, and Seth tackled him into the couch, which was my sign that things were pretty much back to normal. He lucked out. By lunchtime, he was completely back to plain old Seth.

"So, what do we do?" Billy said through a mouthful of hot Spagghettio's. We were on the back porch, eating lunch and kicking rocks as we tried to think our way through this situation.

"Call NASA," I said. "Or the ASPCA."

Seth threw a stick at me, and I ducked. That was fair, I deserved that one.

"Look, we got lucky," I said. "Seth could've gotten stuck that way. This isn't Alice in Wonderland guys, this is life and death. This thing is WAY bigger than us. We need to give it to the authorities."

Billy snorted, and licked sauce off his chin. "So, they can do what? Make weapons? Human dinosaur hybrid soldiers? Turn their girlfriends into literal Catwoman? What is the government going to do with it that's really any good?"

"Spiderman," said Seth, as though that explained anything.

"What?"

"Spiderman. Doc Connors. The lizard? That's what they would do with it. Try to fix people. But it doesn't work, it just makes monsters. That's why Doc Connors is a…what do you call it?"

"Tragic character?"

"Yeah," said Seth. "It turns out tragic. I think this time Billy is right."

Billy stopped slurping his o's. "I am?"

Seth grinned "Don't get used to it. But yeah, I think this time you're right."

The two of them looked at me. I hated this. I was always the holdout, the quiet one, the 'don't make waves' one, the cautious friend. And in my defense, my cautious nature saved our asses more than a few times. But I knew that this time I was solidly outvoted, with no solid defense other than following the rules. But I don't think anyone ever really wrote down any rules for what to do when you discover space goo that turns people into dogs.

I really don't.

Friday, October 25, 1974

Akona had a reputation for Halloween. Every household jumped headlong into the spirit of the holiday by decorating their front yards for the annual Macabre Manor contest, and by either attending or participating in the town's Halloween Parade. If you were a fan of Halloween, this was the place.

This year, Halloween in Akona did not disappoint. From haunted houses, and cornfield mazes, to haunted hayrides, the week before Halloween was packed with things to do. My dad told me that our traditions date back to the 1920's; the town-wide party was suggested as an alternative to the otherwise nasty tricks of outhouse tipping and turning cows loose. This was definitely better.

A week had passed since our adventure in the woods and Seth's turn as a were-puppy. He didn't seem to have many aftereffects, though I felt sure I saw him shaking his butt once or twice during lunch as though he was wagging a tail that wasn't there. All things considered, we got off *light*, and no worse for wear. The Space Goo was safely contained in a volumetric flask with a cork in it, as tight as I could make it. So far so good.

After school let out, the Neutron Knights took the scenic route home. Normally we would just zip down 7th and take the back alley to my backyard gate, but this week of all weeks of the year was the time to take a long, leisurely ride past the best Halloween houses. We put the brakes on and admired the views.

"Holy crap! How'd the Petersons get that giant tarantula so high on their roof?" gasped Billy. "Its legs dangle past the windows across the whole second story!" He made his own legs and arms wiggle.

Seth nudged my side. "Forget the Petersons, check out the Wilson house. Hanging bodies convincingly from a cobwebby tree gets my vote for the coolest house."

"Feast your eyes at the Taylor's gated arch," pointed Billy, jumping up and down like a circus poodle. "That's a long bony arm hanging over the top and I'll betcha it moves as you walk under it. Absolutely a hundred percent it's gonna move!"

"There's the Wolford house. I swear, it's the only house in the city that never decorates. Look how neglected it is. He should at least make it look like a haunted house, or something," I stated.

"Hey, that's Mr. Rayburn's house!" said Seth.

Mr. Rayburn, our current homeroom and science teacher, was our favorite by leaps and bounds. He always wore suits and sported a shaved head, real Professor X vibes. He allowed research papers on how superpowers might logically work if superheroes were real for extra credit. Total geek-gasm.

"Now this is a house," I said.

When we stopped, the air grew eerily quiet. I even heard Billy swallow. He whispered. "I absolutely don't know what to look at first."

"I know, it's amazing," I whispered back. "The tombstone with his name's a nice touch."

We walked our bikes around the wrought-iron fence where the graveyard lay, and on top of each spike, orange and purple pumpkins smiled their spooky grins.

"Out of sight!"

"Is that the hugest king of all pumpkins you've ever seen, or what!?" Seth asked with bulging eyes. "Blood even drips down its mouth!"

The stripes weren't just bloody, they were goop-ey. Mr. Rayburn used the seeds and pumpkin flesh to ooze with the blood. Fresh jack-o-lanterns lay on the ground and peeked out from beneath its tentacle-like vines, where a fine mist covered an array of smaller pumpkins posed around the King Pumpkin like they were dancing. I was speechless.

Seth shook his head, amazed, "I bet some things might even glow in the dark."

"Dudes, things don't just glow, look closer under the leaves," Billy stepped closer to the fence. "Those're wires and I see beakers like they do something, like explode or maybe foam."

Seth gasped.

"Is that the Creature from the Black Lagoon on the chimney?"

"And those shingles in its mouth—" said Billy, his eyes twinkling. "The bricks raining to the ground! It's more than absolute cool–it's Wolfman cool. AaaoooOOOO!"

"Are you howling? You are so lame." Seth rolled his eyes.

"Just because you can't recognize the most radical monster, doesn't mean you have to take it out on me or on Wolfman."

"You and your stupid Wolfman obsession. Get over it. You are both lame."

Something turned sour then—what was usually friendly banter between Seth and Billy took on an edge that made me shift uncomfortably on my bike seat.

"You are the dog boy, Seth." Billy barked back. "Shouldn't you show your own kind some respect?

"Very funny asshole," Seth shouted. "Or do you just not care that I could have died? Or been stuck like that forever, or—or—or—"

"This sucks!" I interrupted. "We live in the best town for Halloween ever and you nerds have killed my buzz. Both of you please shut up. Let's just go home."

The rest of the bike ride was silent. We still rode slowly to pass each house for admiration, but we kept our enjoyment to ourselves. About two blocks from my house, we crossed a side street smack into the Meatheads.

They were in the middle of a heinous act, grabbing jack-o-lanterns from people's walkways and slamming them down to the ground, smashing them into a bunch of tiny pieces and laughing their stupid heads off. They ripped down cobwebs, bats, skeletons, going house to house and stripping each one.

We all looked at each other with a silent understanding. Both Seth and Billy glanced at me, and I gave a nod of agreement. We knew it was up to the Neutron Knight to save Halloween. We didn't know how we were going to do it, but if we didn't intervene, there was no telling how many houses they would destroy.

We rode up.

"Could you guys suck any more?" Billy was the first to speak, and his courage gave me courage. Knowing that I was on my bike and could pedal my dumb butt out of there at hyperspeed didn't hurt either.

"Yeah, what the hell is wrong with you dingleberries?" I added.

They stood, slowly, like the bad guys in a spaghetti western. Asher wiped pumpkin guts off his hands and onto his jeans. My blood turned cold.

"If it isn't the dweebs of America club. You nerds better get out of here quick, or you're all dead meat." Troy spat as he spoke, and the glob of spittle landed in front of Seth. Something about the quivering blob hit a switch in Seth, and he turned red.

"The only dead meat around here are the chunks of beef tucked in the rotten teeth of your hot garbage smelling mouth, you Neanderthal."

Then Seth did the bravest thing I've ever seen anyone do. He dropped his bike and started marching up to the Meatheads.

I would love to say that we were heroes. I would love to say that Seth ripped into Asher, Blake and Troy like God's own watchdog. I would love to tell you anything but the truth, which is that we came out of the fight with two black eyes, two split lips, a few bruised ribs, several scraped knees, one broken bike and three very diminished egos.

The only silver lining was that the commotion drew the attention of Mr. Calderson and his family, the residents of the nearest house we had rescued, and the Meatheads, who rode off without wrecking another. Mrs. Calderson tended to our wounds while Mr. Calderson reported the incident to the sheriff, but we all knew that nothing was really going to be done about the incident. They thanked us with ice packs for our faces and some fresh cookies, and we headed home.

It took us another thirty minutes to go three blocks due to the slow painful walk the rest of the way to my house.

"I hate those assholes so much," Seth huffed through his busted lower lip.

Billy agreed, gingerly exploring his black eye with a cautious fingertip. "I know. They need to be taught a lesson! Just... maybe not by us for a while."

"Yeah, they do, but how?" Seth responded. "Asher is like nineteen because he's been held back a grade three times. Blake weighs at least two-hundred and fifty pounds, and Troy was an ex-football jock that turned stoner and got cut from the team; also held back two grades mind you. They've got us beat in strength and size."

"Oh, they got us beat, alright. Pun intended," I said, waving at the general state of our sad, sorry selves. "But that's because they were dealing with little old us."

An idea had been germinating in my mind since I first saw The Pumpkin King in Mr. Rayburn's yard. The wild cross between pumpkin and monster, the blood mixed with the pumpkin guts, the swirl of mist had lighted an inkling in me that I was now prepared to entertain.

"I have a plan," I said.

That was enough for Seth and Billy.

We laid our traps.

Thursday, October 31, 1974

Plotting, I discovered, takes a lot out of a kid. It took me three rounds with the snooze button before I managed to pull myself out of bed. A nervous excitement sparked in my stomach when I realized what day it was. Trotting down the stairs, my feet hadn't even hit the ground floor yet when dad said, "There you are bud! You almost missed spooOOOkkyy paaancaakkesss! See, it's a ghost!"

"Dad, that's a normal pancake."

"Nah, see, it has spooky eyes!" He pointed at two slightly melty chocolate chips in the middle of the pancake, and we both grinned.

"Scarf these down, go put on your costume, and I'll drive you to school today. I have to run in town to do some errands anyway."

"But, what about after school, dad? Seth and Billy can still come over for our Halloween party, right? I usually ride home with them."

"Well, I'll pick the three of you up after school; it'll prevent another possible run in with the bullies. Let's get you three healed up a little more before you face your adversaries in epic battle again."

"Sure, dad. That would be swell." I said, tucking into the pancakes.

After pancakes, it was time to dress in my costume. As soon as I put on my finishing touches, I heard two long honks from my dad idling in our driveway. It was a fairly quick and easy ride to school. I hopped out of the car at the front school steps to see Seth standing there with a cloak over his face only exposing his eyes.

"Listen to them, children of the night. What music they make!" Seth acted as he threw his cloak off to the side and revealed his fangs with an exaggerated hiss and widened eyes.

"Nice Seth. Wow. Your makeup actually looks believable this year. Did you do it?"

"Nope. Nancy."

"Lucky."

"Shut up man. You'd never have a chance with my sister. She's dating some pre-med college dude," he said dismissively. I shrugged, then did a little twirl in my own costume.

"What do you think?"

"You look great too, man. 'Oh no! Where's your head-oh I'm so scared-please don't hurt me!' It's a classic."

Just then, we heard a long howl accompanied by the repetitive squeaking of a tattered bicycle.

Seth placed his hand on my shoulder, shut his eyes, and winced. "Steven, please tell me that if I turn around, he's not wearing that damn werewolf costume again!" He turned around then threw his hands up and yelled. "Of course you'd show up as Wolfman again, fanboy loser."

"Whatever, bat-boy," Billy retorted as he approached. "You're dressed like Dracula again, jerk. Man! These fangs hurt." When he saw my costume, he spit them out. "Groovy, Steven. The usual headless horseman."

Seth gave me a wink. "Does Scooby need a leash and muzzle or are we taking risks tonight?" he said pointing at Billy's wolfman costume.

"Leash and muzzle? You're the dog-boy! You Milo reject." said Billy angrily. "Hey, Steven, do you know why Dracula has no friends? Because he sucks! You get it?" Seth turned and flipped Billy off. I sighed.

"Well, Happy Halloween, my knights." I declared. "Remember, we only wore these tired old costumes to execute our plan. Meet here after school. My dad will take us to my house. Then the fun begins."

Seth looked at me, and I could see the conflict in his face. "Are we sure we want to do this?"

"If you're going to back out, the time is now."

Billy, who ten seconds ago would have happily clocked Seth, now put an arm around his shoulders. "It's okay man. Stevie wouldn't have even suggested this plan if he didn't think it was safe. And he's the scare-diest cat of the three of us."

I shrugged. Billy was right, I was generally captain cautious. But I'd had enough of the Meatheads. If Seth was willing to die for science, how could I not give up as much for justice?

Slowly, reluctantly, Seth nodded. "He hath wrung from me my slow leave…" he said softly to himself. Billy eyed him sideways.

"What was that?"

"Hamlet. Don't you pay any attention in English?"

"What for? I already speak it."

School flew by, full of treats and popcorn and costumes and paying zero attention to anything in class, except for Mr. Rayman's lesson on blacklight and neon. Dad treated us to a quick pre-parade supper of 'Hallo-weenies' (pigs in a blanket with oozy blood red ketchup) before we all started the three-block walk to our parade spot.

The parade did not disappoint. There seemed to be three times the amount of people as the year before. Some of the costumes were cheesy plastic masks, or cute little boys and girls wearing flower, bumble bee, and bear costumes. Meanwhile, some of the older girls wore… very little. In fact, I caught Billy standing facing backwards while the other ninety-nine-point-nine percent of us were watching the parade. He was mindlessly eating popcorn staring at Sandra Slatmore, a local beauty that graduated from our high school four years before we got there, and he made no attempt to hide it. She was friends with Nancy but today she was wearing a small red bikini with devil horns and a tail, and he was staring at her like she was a new blockbuster movie playing on the big screen.

"Dude!" I hissed, nudging him in the ribs.

"I know man, she's—"

"No, dummy, the parade."

"Oh, yeah, parade, right…"

The parade over, it was time for the trick or treating to begin. We waved goodbye to our parents and started to dissipate into the crowd.

"Home by ten!" my dad shouted after us, and I waved a hasty acknowledgement.

Right off of Main there was an alley behind a meat market

named Akona Meats. We broke away from the costume crowd and huddled between the garbage dumpster and a pile of wood pallets.

"Okay knights! Do you have them?" I asked.

"I totally found a dead bat in that cave near Hillsdale. I figure that would be pretty gnarly" Seth stated. "What about you guys?"

"I heard about a huge Gray Wolf that got struck and killed on highway 10. I overheard it on my dad's radio—I rode out there and was able to get some hair off this clump of guts that was—"

"DUDE!"

"I could not pass on the opportunity! I've dreamt about this my whole life; I was born to do this!"

"Wow, a bat and a wolf. Cliche much?"

"Yeah, I guess so." Seth said with a chuckle. "I guess we're that cliché."

"Well, what's yours?" Billy asked, annoyed. "What's so cool that you have deigned to come down from your throne to join us poor lowly cliches?"

"Jumping Spider."

Billy's face dropped, knowing he'd been bested, and Seth grinned widely, enjoying the moment.

"Yeah, okay that's stupidly cool…"

We stood, the buzz of our excitement fading into nerves with a side order of fear. It suddenly seemed to me that we were very small against the backdrop of the stars; our grand plans of revenge coming off as planned was about as likely as another meteor falling in the woods. I did my best to shake it off, and reached into my pocket, passing two small glass Avon perfume bottles to Seth and Billy.

"What the hell is this?"

"It's the goo."

"No, I mean *this*," Billy snorted, holding up the perfume bottle shaped like a cowboy boot.

"It's an empty perfume bottle. We broke most of my test tubes okay, it's not like I can just pick those up at the grocery store! Besides, test tubes look suspicious."

Seth held up his bottle, shaped like a glass horse, and whinnied. Billy doubled over with laughter. It was just what we needed to break the tension.

"I washed them, okay? It's fine. Put your stuff in the bottle and…I guess shake it a little."

I pulled out my own bottle, shaped like a butterfly. Even Seth barked out a laugh at the delicate pink wings on my bottle. I had taken one for the team this time. I popped the leg I'd pulled off the dead jumping spider I found in the basement and tried not to gag at the thought of drinking it. If everything went right, I would be a lot closer to a spider than drinking its leg…

We tightened ourselves into a circle, faces pale but expressions determined in the darkness. It was time.

"We are three," I intoned, beginning the oath of the Neutron Knights. It had been silly fun when we were younger, but now in the dark of a Halloween night, it felt heavy with gravitas.

"We are the triangle, points and sides, strongest of the ancient geometry," murmured Billy, as serious as I had ever seen him in his life.

"We are prime, created of one and two, whole as three, the first number of the first pattern," said Seth, his voice gaining strength. We held out our bottles together in the center, locking eyes.

"We are the triple covalent bond, our hearts are true, our minds are keen, our friendship unbreakable! We are the Neutron Knights!"

As though on some unseen cue, we all drank the potion together. There was an instant thickness that slid down my esophagus and hit my stomach hard. I had been given a sip of some grown-up drink at my cousin Carl's wedding, and this felt like that, times a thousand. We waited, looking at each other for some sign of change, like the Avengers waiting for the Hulk.

THE HULK!

"Crap! Our clothes! Quick, get out of your costumes so they don't tear. We'll need them when this wears off." With a jolt of recognition, Billy and Seth didn't even think twice about stripping down.

I'm not going to say I believe in fate—I don't know enough to know what I don't know, let alone make sense of the things I do know. But the way the rest of the evening shook out, well…

We thought that we were the hunters tonight. Little did we know that we were also the hunted. We were almost nude when a familiar voice rang out.

"Look! They're all getting naked together!" A familiar voice rang out.

Asher.

"I knew it! I knew it!" Troy crowed in triumph. They came speeding up on their bikes and showed no signs of slowing. "Kick them over and take their clothes!"

The Meatheads picked up speed toward us. There was nowhere and no time to run.

I turned to face them and took Troy's boot to the chest, my feet flying up over my head. It had only been two weeks since the last time I thought, chagrined. Then Seth took Blake's rubber sole to the face beside me, and down he went like a sack of potatoes.

The boot came for Billy next, but that's when the evening really took its first turn. Instead of taking a kick to his chest, he caught foot in mid-air. The force with which he grabbed the foot was so strong that it stopped the bike dead in its tracks. Everyone froze.

Everyone except Billy. He lifted the foot above his head, easily taking the rest of Asher with it. This should not have worked for two reasons—one, it would have required superhuman strength. Two, Asher was a solid two feet taller than Billy.

Was. Past tense.

Just then Billy's fingers started to distend and sharp nails tore through the tips of them. I winced as they also shot through Asher's leg. Fur sprouted all over his hands and arms as they thickened in size. We were transfixed, all of us staring silently at the transformation—including Billy, who watched his bulging arm like a three-year-old at the Disneyland Parade; absolute joy and bliss ran across his face. Although we were soon to follow, I remember thinking how horrifying he had looked. It wasn't long before that five-foot two kid became a seven-foot, terrifying werewolf.

"He's a werewolf! HE'S A WEREWOLF! Help meeeeee!" Asher screamed and thrashed, twisting uselessly in Billy's grip. The rest of us had our attention elsewhere.

Seth yelled in pain and dropped to his knees on the asphalt. He was hunched over in a ball with his hands over his eyes, and everyone except Asher snapped their gaze to his back, which started pulsing and bulging as if something was trying to get out. With a wet ripping noise, a spiky black wing pierced through his back, then another. The wingspan was immense. He rose back to his feet which has become two thick claw-like talons protruding from what was left of his green canvas high tops, with a third sticking out of the back. I felt a little sorry for him—he loved those shoes. Troy and Blake had dropped their bikes in awe and terror, unaware that this was just the beginning of the nightmare fuel.

When Seth finally lowered his hands, we couldn't see his face—what there was had been horribly deformed. His nose was swollen and wide, as though he had been stung by hundreds of bees, but the center of his face had collapsed inward like an upside-down heart. His lips had dissolved exposing a row of razor-sharp teeth. His ears were two massive half cone shapes, turning this way and that atop his head. His eyes were large solid black circles that seemed to be glowing blue from the reflection of the neon sign. An unholy screech tore its way out of his throat and into the night. *He may have just taken the crown for the scariest thing I have ever seen.*

The Meatheads must have agreed, because now they had remembered how to scream, and were trying to untangle themselves from their downed bikes to run away. Too late.

Memories are tricky things when you're in pain. I remember shaking violently and the feeling of stinging as two large, segmented spears split the skin on each side of my hips. After that, all I have is vague impressions taken from other people's descriptions—all I knew was the pain. A second pair of thick, hairy appendages sprouted from the back of my lower ribs, a third pair from just under my armpits, and the final pair from my shoulders. My skin felt heavy and hard, almost as though I had rolled in tar and gravel.

The worst thing I remember is my vision widening and… *dividing*, just before two large spikes tore through my face just above my mouth. I found out later that there were two, but in my swimming vision there were eight. Eight of everything. Eight of my jaw got ripped away as the spikes grew larger and curled under where my chin used to be. Then the pain receded, and I tried to adjust to my new vision.

I couldn't see myself and hoped that I looked like something from nightmares. If I looked even half as scary as Seth or Billy, I would be very content. Standing tall, I looked down at the bullies on their bikes and Asher, who had stopped flailing around but was still upside-down, only now frozen in fear; a distinct smell of urine permeated from him, a steady stream of yellow fluid flowing down his shirt, around his cheeks, and dripping from his hair.

I cherish that image to this day.

"Run!" Troy croaked out as Blake scrambled onto his bike. Troy gave up and started hoofing it, but Blake fought gravity like a wild thing and was up and off on his bike. Without hesitation, Seth took to the sky like a bat out of hell. Literally. He was like a giant gargoyle, wings so massive they generated a wind stream when they flapped. He rose and rose and rose into the air, until I had to wonder what he thought he was doing—Blake was getting away! But with a screech he dove, snatching Blake right off of his bike in his giant talons. He executed a neat turn in the air and dropped Blake back to the gathering with a little dramatic flair of his leathery wings. He looked at me with the black pools of his eyes and I startled in eight different places. Troy!

Troy was mine! I started to run. I was traveling so fast with the strength and length of my newly formed legs that I was gaining on him, even with him tearing away at full bore. I was still a little way off, but I had been dreaming all day about one very important science fact; jumping spiders can jump over one hundred times their own body length. I was massive.

So, I jumped. I overshot Troy by at least a hundred feet, which gave me all the fun of running directly toward him in all my hairy arachnid glory. I was starting to make enough sense of my vision that I could watch from several different angles as Troy processed everything that was about to happen. At that moment he was speeding towards me with no ability to stop in time. He struggled to stop, and cartoon-like tumbled straight at me and finally came to a halt directly underneath me. I thought about biting him but decided against it—there was no way to know what ten-foot jumping spider venom would do to your garden variety high school bully. Probably kill him. Not that he didn't deserve it, but I had enough on my conscience for one night. I decided the next best thing would be to wrap him in a web.

"Whhhaatt are ooo dooinng" Billy tried to say through a mouth full of teeth like Bowie knives.

Trying to figure out how my butt works, I wanted to say, but all I could do was click my mandibles and search my spider brain for the answer while Troy went to pieces underneath me. Ah! That was it—I figured it out. I reached down a shorter, but stronger front leg, and picked up Troy, spinning him gently in the air and wrapping him like a bad Christmas present in my sticky web. All tied up, I dragged him back to the crowd.

"Please, don't kill us! We will never mess with you guys again! I swear!" Troy begged.

"Ooo i-ttle, Ooo ate!" Billy muttered with a deep growl. Seth looked at us and opened his mouth, but only a high-pitched screech came out.

Great. We couldn't communicate. I stomped a…(foot?) in frustration, before the answer came to me.

I reached over with a long middle leg and knocked Blake's hat off his head. Then I pointed to the piles we had made of our costumes.

"Ooo ate 'ats?" Billy tried.

I pointed again. Seth picked up the idea and began to strip Blake's jacket from his shoulders. Blake started screaming again. Asher it seemed had greyed out. I gestured to Billy to start stripping him down too.

"Ewww! E's overed en iss!"

I did the best shrug I could with four of my shoulders, and set to work on Troy, who had reverted to crying for his mother.

In the end, it took the better part of an hour to spin a web across Mason Street. We had intended for Main Street, but there were just too many people for me to get around safely. I picked two big oak trees on opposite sides of the street and strung a huge web across them. Billy tied their clothes into knots, while Seth picked them up one by one and dropped them neatly onto my web. They hung there, exhausted, hoarse, and wearing tighty whities that were a lot tighter than they were white. Billy tossed their clothes into the lower part of the web and dusted his hands on his furry torso. It was a job well done.

"You can't leave us here like this, you freaks. Let us go!" Troy demanded. We just laughed as we slipped into the night. Someone would find them. Eventually. Probably.

We looked at each other, a silent question hanging between us. *What now?*

Seth took the lead. With a soft screech, he lifted off into the night, and Billy and I followed on the ground. We leapt and raced and howled and laughed in our hearts, reveling in our amazing powers. Billy howled until he had nothing left in the tank, and I tested the limits of my jumping and swinging abilities. Let's just say, it doesn't quite work the way it does in *Spiderman*.

Above us, all night, we could see Seth diving and twisting in the air like some beautiful hellkite, his wings spread wide. That's how I remember him best—soaring on borrowed wings across a Halloween sky.

Before long we stopped for breath on the edge of the woods. Billy waved us close, and I realized that he had managed to keep a fanny pack on. Ha! I made a note to tease him about it later. I never did, though. He pulled out a polaroid camera and waved us into the frame. There was a bright flash and a click of the shutter and out shot that iconic white square. I was thrilled—I would get to see what I looked like as a spider! It was everything I had hoped for or dreamed of.

It took four hours for the potion to wear off. Slowly, sadly, we returned to normal. At least that part hurt a lot less. Exhausted, thrilled, full of our victory, we re-dressed in our original costumes and returned to my house for our customary Halloween slumber party. However, there was no sleeping that night. We just kept passing around that Polaroid, gushing about how we felt and how terrifying we all looked. We kept the other Polaroid, the one we took of the Meatheads in their web, hidden under the second cushion of my basement couch. Bully insurance.

On that one night, we were no longer the Neutron Knights, the nerds, the dweebs, the pit stains asking for a knuckle sandwich. That night, we felt like kings. The Kings of Halloween, 1974! And that's exactly what we wrote on the bottom of that Polaroid.

Wednesday, October 30, 2024

The old, faded photo passed from hand to time roughened hand, just as it had the night we took it.

"I loved that night. Do you guys remember?" I asked, passing the photo to Billy.

"Absolutely, one hundred percent. Do you remember how the whole town thought those guys were batshit crazy when they went to the sheriff and tried to blab that we were supernatural bloodthirsty creatures?" Billy asked.

"Yeah. And when that didn't work, they hid outside of my basement window and overheard us talking about the goo."

"That was the meanest, most awesome thing you ever did, giving them a dose," said Seth, smiling softly.

"I would have done better if there had been more time, but pig, frog and slug worked out okay. Remember how Asher got his tongue stuck on a clothesline?"

"Lucky it wasn't a powerline, that dumbass," snorted Seth.

"Didn't Troy win best hog in the County Fair?" Billy responded. We laughed like children, which caused Seth to start a coughing fit.

His breath wheezed, that broken kazoo sound that I hated, but Seth still grinned. "Those were some of the best times of my life."

The beeping of a heart monitor kept time like a metronome. Seth sat up in his hospital bed and gasped with a wince. "Lung cancer sucks! I don't recommend it. Zero out of ten guys."

"I know, man," I said. I grabbed for his right hand, struggling to find it through the tears breaking up my vision. Billy grabbed his left. Seth's skin felt like thin paper and his hands were cold to the touch. He must have mustered up what little strength he had left to squeeze our hands so tightly.

"Thank you for being here with me in the end, guys. I love you two." Seth could hardly choke up the words as thin waterfalls stemmed for the corner of each of his eyes.

"A triple covalent bond, our friendship is unbreakable," I reminded Seth. "Neutron Knights forever."

"I just wish we were young again. Relive some of our old

adventures instead of waiting for my last breath and having you guys see me like this."

"Well, dogboy. You are really old. You're like over two-hundred and fifty in dog years." Billy chimed in with a sneer that instantly melted into a smile.

"Whatever, fartsniffer."

"Funny you should say that, Seth." I said, raising the ghost of a grin for my friend. "Tomorrow is Halloween…and I figured you didn't have a costume or anything." I reached into my pocket and pulled out three small green glowing vials. "Want to go as a bat again?

Both men, old men, my best friends, looked at me in amazement. The years fell away from their faces in the glow of the space goo. Billy raised his head and howled.

"Okay Mid-life-crisis wolf, knock it off," chuckled Seth. "You'll bring the charge nurse down on us."

We looked at each other. There was nothing else to say. Gnarled hands took hold of small glass vials, a little bit of bottled childhood.

That following night we gave that old photo a sibling, titled *The Kings of Halloween, 2024.* Just a picture of a few monsters to anyone else, but to us it was a family photo. That was the last night we rolled as a trio.

Every year we visit Seth's grave on Halloween. We sit with him sharing stories of our adventures, our kid's adventures, his grandkid's adventures. He'd be proud of them, and I hope, of us. I wipe the dew off the lettering on his headstone. *Seth Rogenstein. Beloved Husband, Father, and Son. Neutron Knight.*

Well, that last story really pierced me
to the heart- it was a real fear jerker.
I'm so glad it made the cut! Now on to a
poem I'd like to serve you. It's been a
while since I've recited a poem…but let
me take a stab at it.

Jacko

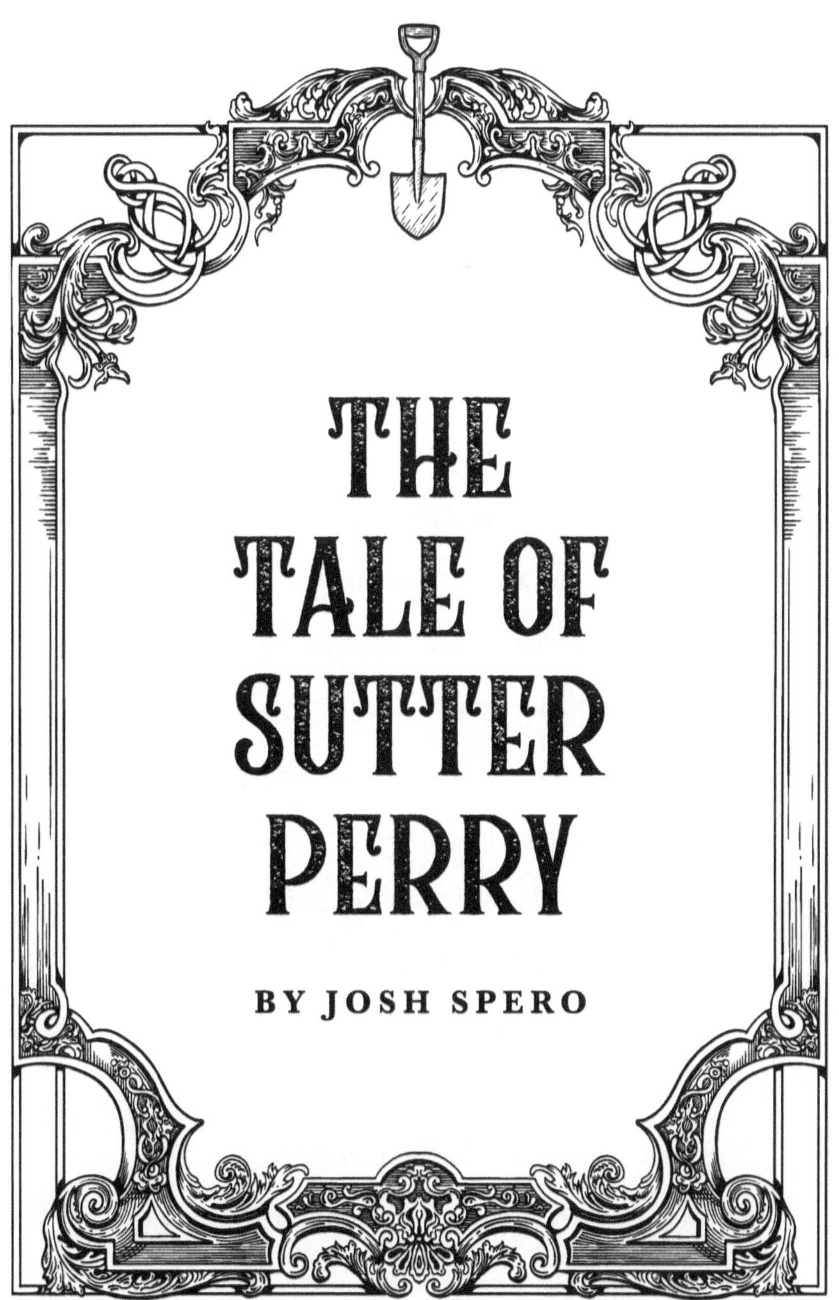

THE TALE OF SUTTER PERRY

BY JOSH SPERO

Here's the tale of Sutter Perry

Who loved to stroll the cemetery,

Searching for all the recently dead

To dig them up for his use instead.

If the body was fresh, he'd get real excited

As seasonal décor, it made him delighted!

For Halloween, he'd go all out

And strew the corpses all about.

Through his yard and his garden and wrapped around trees

The limbs and the torsos would dance in the breeze.

Sometimes if he felt especially merry,

He'd add someone's head like a maraschino cherry.

All of the townsfolk thought he was a faker—

Disguising himself as a master prop maker,

So every year they'd all gather to see

His ghastly display on his Halloween spree.

Alas, the spectators, if they only knew

The unholy endeavors he'd secretly do

So you'd better not die, for when they come to view

His next Halloween prop, it just might be YOU!

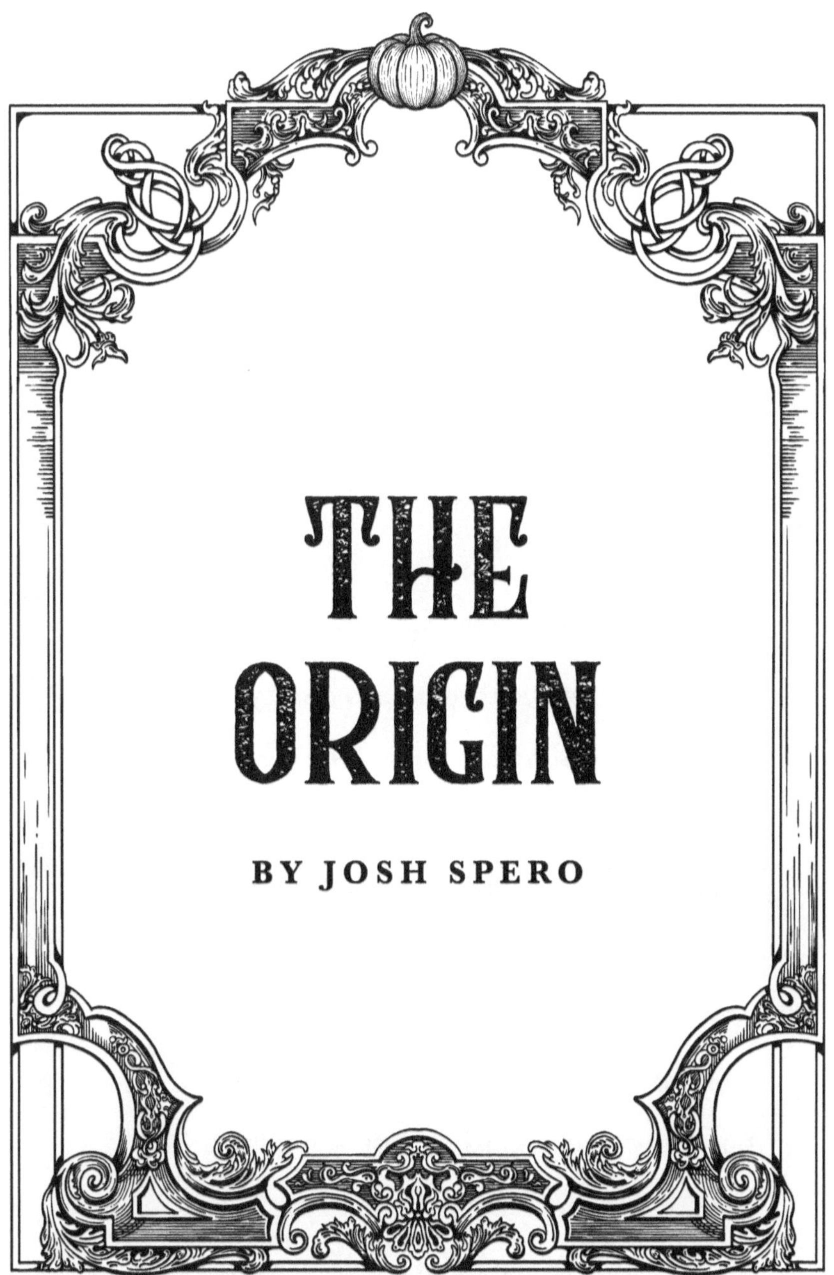

THE ORIGIN

BY JOSH SPERO

The knife it went in, and the knife it went out.

The slick orange flesh was strewn all about.

The brown stem was prickly and easy to grab,

To pierce the round top, he plunged a hard stab.

Lost in the moment, he sliced, and he diced

Johnny did not stop till he felt it sufficed.

But in his excitement, he twisted and slipped,

In the forehead was stuck the knife he had gripped

His perfect attempt was now ruined and marred,

Smack dab in the center the pumpkin was scarred.

Still, Johnny refused to give up in dismay,

He believed that mistakes were just chances to play.

Instead, Johnny thought, let's make him unique

I think I can save him with one little tweak

I'll cut a third eye, that'll make people shriek

And if people object, who needs their critique?

So Jacko, the triple-eyed pumpkin was made

But this was no pumpkin to just be displayed.

"You're my best friend," said Johnny to Jacko's round face,

And proceeded to take him all over the place.

Everywhere Johnny went, Jacko was there

Trying to drum up the best ways to scare.

Pulling gruesome pranks was their favorite past time

Though once in a while they'd cross that fine line

Between good-hearted fun and something too mean,

But Jacko and Johnny would never come clean.

After a while Jacko grew old

And most of his flesh slowly rotted to mold

But Jacko transcended his pumpkin-head start,

He made himself real, in young Johnny's heart.

An invisible friend always ready to play,

Jacko and Johnny would laugh through the day.

Until one sad evening our young Johnny died

 Tears soaking his grave where the townsfolk had cried,

And unknowingly watered a small pumpkin seed,

That started to sprout midst the bracken and weed.

It sprouted some roots and a black leafy vine

And over the year it grew so divine!

It started to bear a strange orange fruit

Like a pumpkin, but this had a much thicker root.

The root it grew wider, and tall as a tree,

Pushed up toward the sky for the people to see.

The town was amazed and couldn't explain,

So they adopted the Johnny Tree as its name

Exactly a year after Johnny had died

The whole town gathered from far and wide

To honor his life and remember that night

Around his tree, they held candlelight

But instead of them simply holding a flame,

They held lit Jack-o-lanterns to honor his name.

All together they held them up high

And what they saw next they couldn't deny

They witnessed the greatest miracle of all

The strange fruit emerged and stood up real tall

It unearthed its body that grew from the grave,

Rumbling the ground like a thunderous wave.

It was hard to ignore its towering size

Or the round orange face with the three glowing eyes.

The Halloween spirit had made him as real,

As the ghoulish delight Halloween lovers feel.

He became the Cipher for all that is Spooky,

For all that is joyous and scary and kooky.

Johnny Leopold loved him, so Jacko became

And carried the memory of Johnny's name.

When he had died, his best friend had awoken

On that evening when Johnny's first legend was spoken.

Oh, how the table has turned in the end

Johnny is now Jacko's invisible friend

Together forever, in darkness and light,

The twin laughing figures of Halloween night.

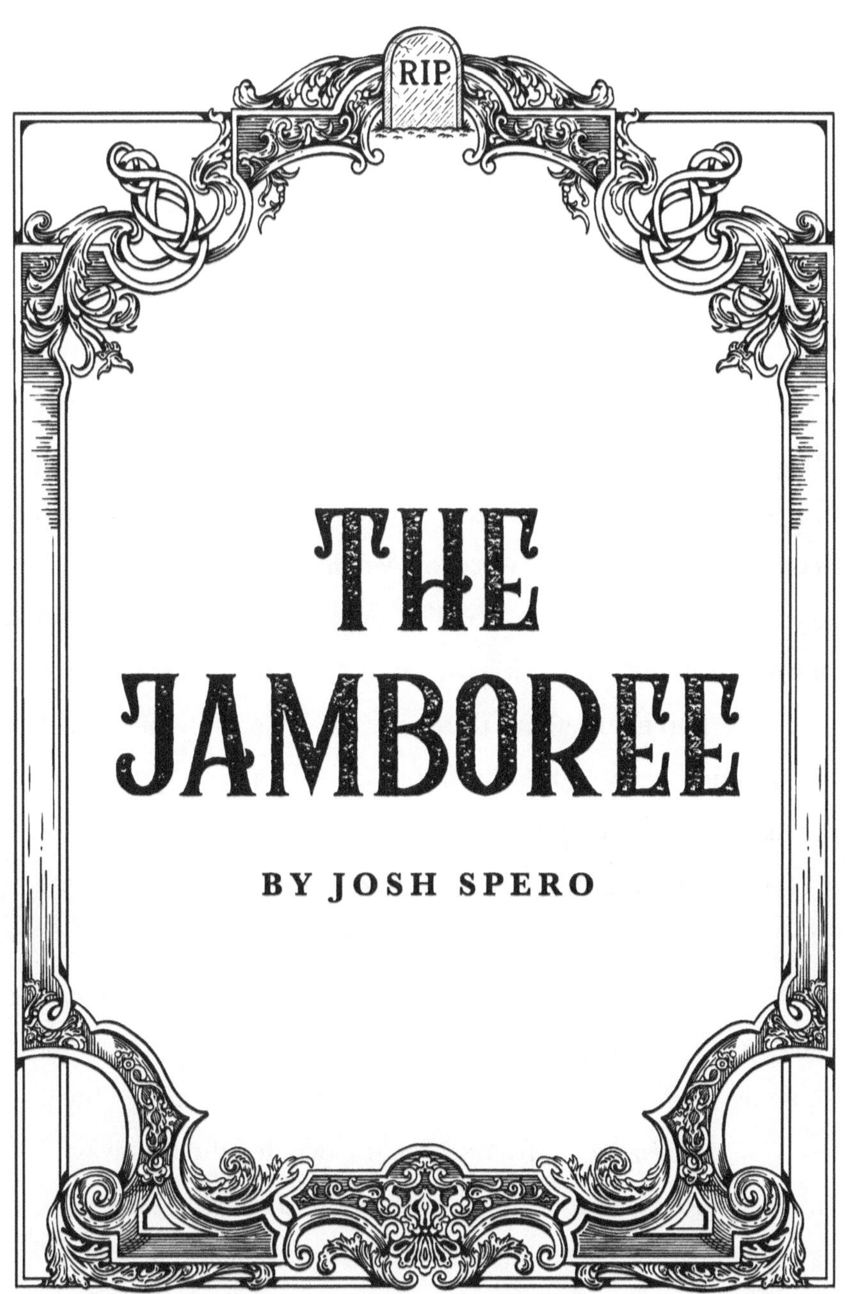

THE JAMBOREE

BY JOSH SPERO

Ella Murray was often described in teacher's notes as 'feisty'. Not in a bad way—you could almost hear the amused sigh as a teacher tried hard to find a word with a gentler connotation, couldn't, and wrote 'feisty' instead. Usually followed by the words 'precocious', 'sweet', or 'kind', as a way to soften the blow. She was, like many children, more interested in *appearing* to be fearless than she was in cultivating any sort of daredevil experiences. Though Ella was always quick to stand up to a challenge or a dare, her natural understanding of consequences made her wary; she would take a dare, but the terms had to be clear and fair. So, it had always been and so, she supposed, it always would be. And so it was…until the year she turned thirteen.

She had heard about thirteen—the edge of the minefield that was High School, puberty, fashion (she had been quietly practicing new make-up techniques while her father had been out on a field study) and the Social Gauntlet. On top of her concerns about turning thirteen in general, Ella was also new to Grant Parish, and she was anxious about fitting in at her new school. Because of her dad's job as a wildlife biologist, they moved around frequently, so making new friends was nothing really new—but these would be *high school* friends. So, she decided the best way to move forward was to set her chin, stand up straight, and be as unapologetically herself as possible. "Be the magnet," her mom would have said. "You'll attract the ones you want and repulse the ones you don't. Just be you with all your gut."

It looked like her magnet was attracting the weirdos.

In fairness, she thought, that wasn't a bad thing. At least these weirdos were really kind, and man were they *interesting*. Ella and her dad had chased his elusive, endangered birds from Seattle to Myrtle Beach, but Louisiana was as different to the rest of America as the deep, dark, mystical swamps were from the wide misty vistas of the West Coast. Louisiana people had a depth to them that other Americans she'd met hadn't…as though there was another layer underneath the skin of a Louisiana native, and if you shone a light brightly enough behind them you might be able to make out the shape of it. She first noticed it when she finally settled on 'The Girls' as her friends, this slippery, ephemeral *something* they all seemed to have twisted around their accents. Especially, she noticed, when they stopped talking about boys, and started talking about ghosts.

It was two weeks till Halloween and stories about "haints" were being passed around like superstar baseball cards. Ella hadn't heard this many ghost stories in one place since her mom used to read her those scary story books when she was a kid. The ones with the pictures that looked like they were painted with spiderwebs and made your eyeballs itch to look at them. It was as though each of her new friends was a whole national repository of urban legends and ghost stories. They were spending yet another lunch hour chewing their slightly stale school pizza and the latest spooky tale.

"Yeah, an' if you don't decorate for Halloween, he comes back an' haunts ya for a whole year. Can y'magine?" said Sara, trying not to chew on the end of her braid but ultimately forgetting.

"Thank goodness we ain't livin up there. Halloween gives me the creeps. I'm tryina stay as far away from ghosts as possible. Plus, my mama says that all ghosts are evil and wanta hurt you," Nancy chimed. Nancy always had to make sure she had a commentary of some kind on every story. Ella suspected it was because she didn't talk much in class; all the thoughts built up and came out of her at the lunch table.

"Ghosts are fine Nancy, it's *haints* that wants ta hurtcha."

"There's no diff'rence. That's what momma says."

"There is so. Prove it t'ya. Is it not true—" said Sara, putting on what Ella thought of as the 'Atticus Finch' voice, "that a house which has been painted haint blue can still be haunted, 'cus haint blue only protects against haints and evil spirits, but not ghosts as a whole?"

"All ghosts are haints."

"Not so. It's like squares and rectangles. All squares is rectangles, not all rectangles is squares."

"So, all haints are ghosts, but not all ghosts are haints?" Ella asked, amused.

"Zactly. See Nan, Ella gets it, and she's a Yankee."

Nancy huffed her annoyance, pushed her glasses up her nose, but conceded the point.

"Don't be salty Nancy. Ghosts aren't real anyways. I mean, no offense, but there's no such thing." Ella said, wanting to restore the peace. It took less than a second to realize that she had stepped on a mine.

The girls both stopped and stared at her, Nancy with wide,

pale eyes, and Sara with a dark look on her freckled face.

"You ain't been to Harrington Cemetery," she said, as though it were an accusation rather than a statement of fact.

"N-no…" said Ella, trying to figure out if she would be able to salvage these friendships if she said the wrong thing. Nancy probably, she was pretty easy going, but there was an edge of steel in Sara that Ella suspected could cut you as soon as shield you.

"Course she hasn't, why on God's Green Glorious earth would she go there?! Just 'cause you think it's the be—and end-all of Gully Bank don't make it so Sara Masterson."

"What's Harrington Cemetery?" Ella asked cautiously, still trying to feel the situation out.

"Only the most haunted cemetery in Grant Parish," said Sara, almost vibrating with excitement. "It was cursed by a witch, but nobody knew it was cursed, so when they tried to hallow the ground for a cemetery, the priest that did the ritual died of a heart attack right there at the gates of the cemetery! And if you go to the cemetery, you'll hear all the voices of the dead on Halloween night, because their souls have to come back year after year until the curse is over."

Ella looked over at Nancy, who was nodding solemnly, and her heart sank.

"S'true," said Nancy, placing a hand on her heart. "I heard them before. I went there with the scouts when I was a kid. Momma was so mad…"

"No, you didn't Nancy Prater. You're a big baby, you'd fall over in a dead faint before you ever set foot in Gully Bank," scoffed

Sara.

"Okay, fine! But my friend, Lucy, did, and she told me everything." Nancy retorted. Sara rolled her eyes and turned back to Ella.

"I'm not saying that the two of you are liars. I just don't believe in ghosts." Ella said, gambling on the response.

Sara eyed her suspiciously and then seemed to come to a decision.

"All right then, sleep the night in Harrington Cemetery. If there's no such thing, you'll be perfectly safe."

"Um, except for the bobcats, raccoons, snakes, alligators, or anything else that bites," said Nancy.

"There is no such thing."

"Then go sleep in the cemetery."

"I'm not big on camping."

Sara grinned and played her trump card, the last ace of the childhood dead man's hand.

"I dare you."

So that was the only way off the land mine—answer a dare. Fair enough

"When do we leave?" said Ella, playing it cool. Nancy shook her head at both of them, but that hard steel look in Sara's eye gave Ella something close to a shiver.

"Halloween, of course."

#   #   #

The next week was spent negotiating the terms of the dare. Nancy was the de facto mediator, which Ella felt gave her a bit of an advantage; she suspected that Nancy both felt sorry for Sara and was a little fed up with her smug glee. Ella did her best to shrug everything off. If this was the price of admission into a group of friends and a level of respect, then so be it, she would deal with the inevitable mosquito bites and boring empty hours waiting for dawn. Which is all that would be there, of course. She was a scientist's daughter, she knew better than to be afraid of the dark. There was nothing waiting in the dark that wasn't there in the light.

"No tent."

"Mosquitos are real. Tents stop mosquitos. Ghosts are not real, but if they were, would a tent stop them?"

"Only if it was a haint blue tent," said Nancy thoughtfully.

Sara sighed and chewed harder on the long grass stalk she had plucked from the edge of the Commons. "No, a tent wouldn't stop a ghost."

"Then I should get a tent."

"Fine. You can have a tent, but no fire. An' no flashlight."

Nancy shook her head "Nope, flashlight is basic safety equipment, she gets a flashlight."

"I can live without a fire."

Nancy added the terms to her spiral notebook page. "Okay, here's what I've got so far. Arrive at the cemetery at 10 PM, gotta stay til dawn, which my phone says is 6:57 AM but we're just gonna call it 7, you can bring a tent, a flashlight, a snack, a water bottle, and a blanket. No electronics, no phone. But you can bring a bible."

"And a crucifix," added Sara. Ella frowned, but Nancy nodded emphatically and added it to the list.

"What do I need that for?"

"You ain't never seen *The Exorcist?*" said Sara, looking affronted.

"No."

"Well, that's a problem," said Nancy. "We're gonna have to fix that, you need to know how to handle these things before you go."

They fixed it that weekend.

Ella was starting to wonder if she was making a mistake.

#   #   #

To Ella's relief, and Sara's disappointment, the cemetery was quite pretty and peaceful looking under the waxing moon. Gully Bank (a town so small that had she blinked during the car ride over she would have missed it) was clearly proud of its one dubious claim to fame. In addition to the various dilapidated "witch" themed items in town— several hand painted wooden witch signs, a tiny four table diner named 'The Cauldron', and an ancient apothecary shop nestled next to the brick 1950's post office— they kept their cemetery neat as a pin. The little dirt paths were in good repair, precisely lined with concrete paving stones, and even the crooked gravestones were clean and uncrumbled. Ella, Nancy, Sara, and her older brother Thomas climbed gingerly out of the ancient truck and stood under the metal archway.

"Looks fine to me," said Thomas with a shrug. "You sure your dad is okay with this?"

Ella swung a backpack over her shoulder and gathered the tent bag under one arm. Dad was okay with anything that didn't disrupt his latest field study. A Halloween sleepover fit that bill. He didn't even ask where it would be, which suited Ella just fine. She could take care of herself.

"Yeah, it's cool."

"I've got his number Tommy," said Sara, covering for her. "He knows where we are."

"Must be a pretty chill guy, your dad."

"Practically an ice cube."

Thomas shrugged again and the four of them stepped cautiously into the cemetery, Nancy bringing up the rear. The headlights of the still running truck cast their shadows long and leaned onto the path and over the gravestones, and Ella couldn't shake the feeling that something wasn't right. This place was *too* nice. Too clean. It looked like a bad movie set.

That's when they saw the *other* cemetery gate.

If the cemetery so far had looked like a bad movie set, then this gate before them was the most genuine, ancient, crumbling, rotted portal this side of hell. Moss dripped from what remained of the cast iron arches, already half powdered into blackish red rust that peppered the ground beneath. One gate swung akimbo from the remnants of a hinge pin that looked like a soft breeze would disperse it into nothing. It creaked like the pressure of some monstrous foot on a groaning floorboard, warning you of the approaching danger. It looked, in short, exactly like the entrance to the most haunted graveyard in all of Louisiana should.

Tommy shook his head. "Nope," he said, turning on his heel. "Absolutely not. Pack up girls, let's get home."

"No!"

"Tommy no, we cain't!"

"We came all this wa—"

"That," said Tommy, pointing an imperious and almost angry finger at the gate "is a bad idea. This over here? This here is fine. Past that gate, huh-uh. I ain't gonna be responsible for some kid gettin' her immortal soul sucked outta her body or some such because y'all thought it would be a hoot to dare her."

Ella lifted her chin like a prize fighter waiting for the blow and pinned the older boy with a cool stare.

"I didn't take you for a coward Tommy."

Nancy gasped, and froze, watching. Sara flinched but kept her gaze steady between her older brother and Ella. Tommy put his hand down, then shook his head.

"I aint' a coward, *cher*, I'm Cajun, and I know *maudit* when I sees it. You think you're brave Yankee girl, but what you are is a damn fool. I ain't goin, and neither is you. *Zwah.*"

"I am going in there. I'm going to stay the night. And if you don't let us, we'll tell everyone that this was your idea, and you made us come out here."

Sara stood next to her, crossing her arms. "I'll tell Pere Costanze that you peed on one of the graves."

Tommy gaped, and Ella thought his eyes would fall out of his head when Nancy joined them, albeit a bit sheepishly.

"It *is* a double dog dare Tommy," she said, pleadingly. "You have to let her do it."

Tommy's face darkened, and he lifted his hand as though to start reaching for them, but Sara piped up.

"I'll getcha a date with Nancy's sister."

He stopped, and they all stared at Sara.

"How?" said Nancy, simply.

"I know she smokes weed an' I'll tell your parents if she doesn't go out with Tommy."

This was apparently a revelation to Nancy, and not necessarily a dealbreaker for Tommy.

"A real date. Dinner an' a movie. No chick flicks."

Sara shook her head. "No dinner, movie, you gotta share a popcorn. Chick flicks are on the table, but I know she likes spooky stuff an' there's a new movie 'bout *rougarus* out come next Thursday, I can put in a good word for ya."

Tommy spat in his hand and offered it to Sara. She followed suit and they shook while Nancy looked on in horror and Ella watched in appreciation of a fellow master negotiator. Yeah, this would be worth it—worth a real, honest to god lasting friendship.

If she survived.

Ella set up shop on a stone bench in the center of the old cemetery. It looked as though nothing but the ancient swamp vines held the slowly disintegrating stone together. She flashed the girls a thumbs up; they had decided that the only one who really needed to go inside the gates was the dare-ee. Tommy had shaken his head and started walking back to the truck.

"Got everything? You okay?" Nancy sounded more nervous than Ella felt, and she felt plenty nervous.

"I'm good. No such thing, remember?"

"R-right," mumbled Nancy.

"*Bonne chance*," said Sara, nodding approvingly. Ella zipped the door of her tent closed, then unzipped the inner lining to reveal the mesh window. The mosquitoes wouldn't get in. She hoped nothing else would either.

"Yeah… Please don't die!"

"See you in the morning Nancy," said Ella, with a wave that was more cheerful than she felt. She heard Tommy say something about crazy Yankees, but he was already too far away to hear clearly. Their voices and the sounds of their steps fell away into the oppressive darkness. Ella shook her head as she watched the lights from their flashlight fade into the distance. She sat, staring out into the murky darkness of the gravestones, and sighed. It was going to be a long one.

She tried to busy herself by unpacking her snacks, arranging her blanket and pillow just so, finding the best angle for her flashlight…but it wasn't long before the night and all of its mysteries crept in. She became achingly aware of each creaking tree branch, the rustle of the Spanish moss as it dragged through the slow breeze, low groaning ribbits from the bullfrogs out in the mist. Did alligators come out at night? She didn't know. She kicked herself for not reading up on it. Each and every sound rang like a bell inside her head, vibrating with possible danger. In her head, she knew there was nothing between her and the quiet of the dead but her thoughts. In her heart, she wondered. Was it the wind? Really? The creatures, the crawlies, the creeping things that slithered from beneath rocks and waited in the dark waters of the bayou for the unsuspecting Yankee, way out of her depth? She gripped her flashlight tighter.

The wind picked up. The branches groaned. She could feel the air moving like a thick slime around her, muggy and chill at the same time. The wind grew louder, and something pricked at the edges of her mind. There was a faint sound like music, but no matter how much she strained, she couldn't catch the tune.

Then she heard the whisper.

"Run."

She shook her head as though to clear it. The sounds of the cemetery had stopped; there was nothing to hear but perfect silence. The hair on her arms stood up as though a current had been run through her body.

"Run from here" the whisper hissed past her ear again. She shivered, glancing at the zipper on the tent.

"The dead live here," came a new sound, dark like cold molasses.

"Leave here or die."

The wind swept through, a mighty gust, and the walls of the tent pulsed in and outward as though a giant hand were squeezing them. She muffled a shriek against her hand.

"Die and join us!" added a new voice, full of cheerful menace.

"Only dead are welcome here. Be gone!"

The silence again, and the ringing of her own heart beating painfully in her ears. She flicked her flashlight from one side of the tent to another, searching for…she didn't know what. Something.

Had she been breathing harder, she wouldn't have heard it, but Ella was an old hand at staying quiet in the dark. In the long years when her mother was slowly dying, when the cancer made her mother's nights long and sleepless, Ella had learned to control her breathing, keeping it quiet and shallow. Now, over the sound of her own quiet struggles, she heard a giggle.

A giggle.

Sara and Nancy. Tommy was probably in on it too.

All of her cold fear boiled over into a moment of white-hot anger. Not at her friends of course, they were doing the most obvious, cliche thing ever. No, now she was mad at herself for even *thinking* about being scared. Of course it was them! What an idiot she'd been. She sat, contemplating her next move. Did she call them out? No. Sara would claim she'd reneged on the bet. Ella wondered if they were watching the tent. How could she get them back without losing the dare? She couldn't leave the cemetery…but she could disappear from her tent. She could unzip the window on the opposite side of the tent and climb out. They'd never see her leave. She could hide out in the stand of trees next to the mausoleum. Then who would be laughing when they came to get her and found nothing but an empty tent?

She surveyed everything she had brought in with her and decided to keep the granola bar and water bottle. Everything else she silently kicked and flailed at, trying to make it look like there was some kind of struggle. She kept her flashlight in her hoodie pocket, so it's movement would look like she was still there. Then she started the slow task of pulling down the zipper. Climbing out, she crouched behind the tent, then flicked off her flashlight. The moon was bright enough to see what she needed to see.

One…two…three…

She screamed, the way the three of them had screamed during *The Exorcist* when that girls' head had gone spinning, and then she ran for it. She only stumbled slightly once before hiding behind the neglected mausoleum. When her friends came out to investigate, she'd jump out and scare them—who would be laughing then?

She sat there waiting behind the stone structure, deathly quiet, straining her ears to hear them in the dark. What she heard was not, by any stretch of imagination, her friends.

"Well, that were simple enough."

A man's voice broke the silence, low and slightly amused. "We didn't even need t'manifest nuffink. Poor li'l fing."

Ella's eyes widened, and she could feel her stomach spinning. That was no local—the voice had some kind of British accent to it, almost like that guy from Mary Poppins.

"Aw-right everyone, we're in th'clear. Let the party commence!"

Party? Here? She started to turn, meaning to peak around the old stone wall, when she heard a spine-chilling shriek. Ella spun around and found herself face to face with an iridescent woman glowing pale, ghostly blue. The woman looked like something out of Ella's history book, dressed head to toe in 1920's finery; a wildly feathered headband drew the eye down to short, choppily bobbed hair, long fringed dress and pearl lavalier, glowing the same wild blue.

They stared at each other, and Ella found that she couldn't breathe as she stared into the blue flames where the woman's eyes had once been.

"Ghost," Ella whispered.

All rhyme and reason drained from her body, and she turned to run—headfirst into the low roof of the mausoleum. There was a sickening crack, a slow *thud*, and Ella's vision went white-ish green before her consciousness went black. She was out cold before her body hit the ground.

# # #

"I'm telling ya, we really ought'ta disappear. She won't remember."

She could feel the pain in her head before she could summon the energy to open her eyes. She decided to keep them closed. If you couldn't see it, it couldn't hurt you.

A woman's voice joined in. It was gentle, if stern in its tone, and it had the same strange sound of being out of time. "Look at her, Able. She needs help. She's just a girl. What if she was Lilly? Would you want somebody to leave her on her own if she was hurt? In the damp, in the middle of a cursed and haunted graveyard, in the middle of the night no less?"

Ella kept her eyes shut. She had bonked her head. This was an… what did they call it…it was hard to think over the pain in her head. Auditory hallucination! That was it! Just an auditory hallucination. That was the situation. The end.

"Elizabeth I don't disagree luv, but wot exactly would y'have me do? She's a bit conkered at the bleedin' moment."

Lying on the ground, Ella slowly opened her eyes to thin slits. There were five blue people all bent over and staring at her with their blue-flame eyes wide and unblinking.

"Go and get the other ones!"

"Wot other ones?"

"The ones that came in the jalopy. They dropped her here."

A new voice joined in. It was a stuffy voice, vaguely irritated, as though lunch was already late and would not be arriving for at least another fifteen minutes.

"They've long since gone, Elizabeth, back to the town one might expect."

Ella heard the woman sigh, and tried to focus in on her face, but she had stood up and was too far away to be more than a blue glow. The slight movement of Ella's head did not go unnoticed.

"Blimey, she's awake! Come on darlin', sit yerself up, let's have Dr. Halverd have a look at'ya. Don't fret now, there's a girl, up y'get."

She felt something like cold fur around her shoulders, and she did her best to open her eyes as she was propped against the wall of the mausoleum. She shook her head slowly, trying to get a grip on the pain, and opened her eyes as much as she could.

There were not five ghosts; there was a cemetery full. In fact, there were so many that the glow of their flaming blue eyes drowned out the moonlight and bathed everything in a spectral glow. All of them stood in silence, waiting for a reaction from her.

She obliged them by passing out again.

The stuffy voice was back, but it had a calm, professional feel to it now.

"Concussed, surely. Would that I had some laudanum about my person; I could at least treat the incredible headache she must be suffering. But you needn't concern yourselves overly, she will of course live."

Ella opened her eyes. The blue face nearest hers was old, wrinkled, and annoyed, but not unkind. It nodded and stepped back from her.

"See? Perfectly viable little specimen."

That got her attention. She knew what her father did with his specimens.

"Please, don't hurt me!" she said, feebly holding her arms up in front of her. The pain was bearable, but it still made the world a bit swimmy. The blue glow of the…people…didn't help.

"Hurt ya? We saved ya!"

She turned toward the voice. A young, scruffy looking man in what she thought of as maybe old-style cowboy clothes crossed his translucent arms, his duster flapping in a non-existent breeze. This one must be Able then, she thought.

"Who are you all?" Ella asked with her head on a swivel. "Are you ghosts? Are you all from this graveyard? Are you under the curse? Why are you talking like—"

"I preferred her unconscious, I think," said the elderly man, and the flapper girl smacked his arm lightly in admonishment.

"What makes you fink we're gonna tell ya? You're not even

s'posed t'know we exist!" Able retorted. "You was meant to run off, yeah? But, nah, ya ran yer bonce right into the wall, so 'ere you are then. You've got a bit of spunk to ya. I'll give ya that. Here, let's see if I can help y' up."

Able squatted and held out his hand. Ella reached out and grabbed it. That feeling of cold fur returned. Not only was she able to grab him, a strange and tingling sensation seemed to shoot between the two of their hands like mini fireworks on the surface of her skin. He helped her up and she slowly looked at all of the faces of the huge assembly, all staring at her like she was the ghost, and they were the living.

"How d'ya do? Name's Able, luv." He shook the hand he was still holding.

"Oh, um, Ella. Sir."

Able grinned at that and gave her a cheeky wink. The flapper girl rolled her eyes and took Ella's other hand along with her attention.

"Hello, Ella. My name is Elizabeth Sommers, but you can just call me Mrs. Sommers. At least, that's what my students used to call me. Welcome to the Harrington Cemetery Halloween Jamboree!"

Elizabeth smiled warmly, and Ella felt a little better. A teacher? Sure, why not, why wouldn't teachers be ghosts.

Elizabeth glanced up at Able with her eyebrows raised as if to ask a question without speaking. Able looked at Ella, then back at Elizabeth, with a little shrug.

"Well, how about it, luv? Care to join us?"

A murmur spread throughout the crowd. Ella couldn't tell if

it was angry or not.

"Oh, pipe down you lot!" The murmur quieted.

"I shouldn't think," said the elderly man, "that this is not a particularly good idea, you two. The living are not meant to 'hob nob' with the dead, as you say."

Elizabeth put a friendly arm around the girl. "Come now Harold," she said, cajoling. "You yourself said we should keep a close eye on her until the rest of the living arrive. She can't just sit here all night against the mausoleum. Able and I will keep her out of mischief."

Another murmur rippled among the assembly.

Harold sniffed and cleaned a pair of glasses on a ghostly handkerchief. "Do as you like," he said. "But I want it known that I advised against it!"

Elizabeth smiled and turned to say something to Ella, but a cry from the crowd interrupted.

"Wait a minute!" a man's voice rang out. Pushing his way through the spirits was a well-to-do man in the remnants of a fine suit, a top hat, and a handlebar mustache.

"Before she accepts, we must read the 7th and 9th articles from the great Ethereal Accords. She must accept these terms before she may join us."

"But Mr. Weatherton, she's…" Elizabeth turned to Ella, "well, how old are you dear?"

"Thirteen."

"She's only thirteen. How can she agree to terms?"

"Life and death know no age. If she can understand, she can

accept" Weatherton retorted. Just then he waived his hand through the air and pulled a scroll from apparent nothingness. He unwound the scroll and pulled a monocle from the inside of his coat chest pocket.

The old fuddy-duddy, wrapped in layers of moth-eaten tweed, lifted the ancient scroll with trembling, bony fingers. The paper was covered with looping intricate letters that looked like a spider had written it with a golden pen. He shoved it unceremoniously into her face, and she blinked, trying to decipher what could've been a Shakespearean sonnet—or a demonic incantation. Her eyes strained to find meaning, but most of it slipped through her understanding.

"I'm sorry, but I can't—"

"Oh, for pity's sake, listen closely."

Weatherton didn't take a breath—she supposed he no longer needed to—and began to rattle off a litany of 'the signatory shall's,' and 'under the terms of these agreements' and 'the aforementioned' that left her head spinning. After reading the myriad rules and regulations, Weatherton paused and stared at Ella, looking through his monocle with a magnified and unblinking eye of blue fire. He shifted his feet in annoyance, awaiting her response.

"Well, what say you?" he asked as he leaned in a little further over Ella.

Time seemed to hold its breath. Ella just stared. The silence was thick and lingering uncomfortably until a sharp voice cut through it like a blade.

"Bloody hell!" Able barked, tossing his arms up. "Alright, luv. Here's the deal."

He sauntered up beside the old man, brushing cobwebs from his ghostly shoulder.

"Let's skip the theatrics, yeah? Here's what you really need to know."

He raised a translucent finger and began counting them off:

"One. You don't tell anyone about tonight. Not your mum, not your mates, not even your diary. We're not some Halloween party trick, got it?"

"Two. We're bound to the cemetery. Like ghosts on a leash. Only you can party with us—don't go bringin' tagalongs."

"Three. The stories of the dead? They're ours. Share 'em without permission, and you'll learn why they buried us with 'em."

"Four. No mixing life with death. Don't mess with the veil. No spells, no seances, no resurrection foolishness."

"Five. Don't dig up graves or nick trinkets. You want a keepsake; we'll give you one. Steal from the dead, and we'll take more than your breath."

"Six. Don't fall in love with any of us. It's unnatural. It never ends well. Trust me."

"Seven. If you betray us, break the pact, or defile our resting place—we will haunt you. Forever."

"Eight. No touching—unless we let you. Otherwise, we'll pass right through, and it'll feel like plunging your hand directly into a snowbank."

He paused, eyes narrowing. "Finally, if you break any rule... both the living and the dead will pay the price. So, there you have it, luv. Do we have an accord?"

Ella hesitated, the weight of the supernatural pact pressing on her small shoulders.

"Yes, we have an accord," she said, her voice stronger than she expected.

Able whooped with joy, spinning an impressive pirouette. "You heard the lass! Let's get on wiv' it! We're burnin' moonlight!"

The old man with the scroll quietly sifted back into the crowd, and with a sudden, electric jolt—the cemetery erupted as the jamboree commenced.

From beneath the heavy hanging moss of a small grove of trees a band began to play, their instruments gleaming like silver phantoms under the moon, ready to erupt all the sounds of New Orleans' finest jazz. The brass section raised their horns to the heavens, silhouettes gleaming blue against the night sky. The drummer kept time atop a crumbling headstone, while the upright bass player leaned casually against an angel's wing, plucking out deep, resonant notes. Ghosts spun and twirled through the graveyard, some rising above the tombstones in joyful flight.

"Who wants some spirits' spirits?" a ghost called out, and laughter and cheers rang out through the crowd. Phantom glasses clinked in mid-air as bottles floated by, sloshing with glowing liquid. One glass drifted toward Ella's hand. The second it touched her fingertips—

"No, no, no!" Elizabeth materialized from nothing, snatching the drink away with a dramatic swoosh. "That's Sanguis Mortuus— Blood of the Dead. A drink only for us. Poison to the living. Plus, you're far too young to drink. Nice try though." Elizabeth winked at

Ella and disappeared in a burst of blue mist.

Ella's eyes swept across the graveyard in wonder. To her left, five cowboys sat hunched around a table, cards in hand, the scent of tobacco lingering in the air. One tipped his hat at her, tossed his cards on the table, and vanished with a wink. To the far right she saw a beautiful woman who looked like she was completely engulfed in continuous flame. Blue and flickering, it seemed not to have any effect on her—leaving no smoke, and no burns. She sat serenely beside a woman who was all wrinkles and bones, barely distinguishable from the grave itself—except for the faint, icy glow that pulsed from her like a heartbeat.

The rest of the dead danced with feverish joy, their feet stirring no dust, their laughter echoing like music from another realm. They looked like they were having the time of their lives (or, she supposed, their deaths.)

On the outskirts of the revelry, a group of soldiers huddled together, smoking cigars and roaring at old jokes. They were dressed in military uniforms, some tattered and some pristine, which Ella quickly recognized as the Civil War era. With the bluish glow, it was impossible to identify colors or which side they must have fought on... She wished she had paid more attention in social studies class.

But something peculiar-which was very relative, given that she had just watched a phantom bartender mix a drink inside his own skull-—was a soft, green glow. Far off behind the Civil War casualties, one soldier stood apart; rigid, solemn, his back turned to the celebration. What stood this spirit apart even further was his distinct color, a sickly green against the other ghosts' romantic blue, which made his solitude even more ominous. An unsettling chill crept along Ella's spine as she watched him. While laughter and cheer danced in the air, he remained a stark contrast—a dark stain smeared across the vibrant canvas of merriment, like a hole in a stained-glass window.

Able materialized before Ella, enveloped in a shimmering blue glow that obscured her gaze from the shadowy corner she had been fixated on. "How are you likin' the party luv?"

He followed her gaze and shook his head a bit. "Ah," he said, his voice a warm mix of reassurance and mischief. "Don't fret about him. He's harmless s'long as y' steer clear of him, really, just lost in his own world. It's a pity—one magical night each year t'revel and connect, and yet he chooses to sulk away in solitude. But to each their own! Some spirits are too far gone to be redeemed. Now, let's return to the festivities! Can y'jig?"

"Jig?"

"Aye, jig!"

"No…"

"Well, we'll soon fix that."

With a grin Able swept her back into the vibrant chaos of the celebration as the music enveloped them once more.

She did in fact learn to jig. Elizabeth taught her to Lindy Hop, and a graceful pair of spectres in tuxedo and wedding gown waltzed past them to music only they could hear. Jazz gave way to blue grass shifted into Delta Blues transformed into soft romantic ballads of times gone by, eras that Ella couldn't begin to guess at.

She also learned to play five card stud poker from a cowboy named Stuckey who had bet the ranch on a single hand and won the jackpot. His newfound fortune landed him incredible wealth and a beautiful wife.

"Unfortunately," Stuckey said, chewing the end of a cigar and letting the smoke drift out of the neat little bullet hole that sat dead center in the crown of his Stetson, "when the money ran out, so did my wife and my luck."

He and the other cowboys whooped when she drew a Dead Man's Hand of Aces and Eights. Grinning, he handed her a poker chip. It was heavy in her palm and gleamed faintly where the numbers were limned in gold filigree. "Keep it missy," said Stuckey, tipping his hat. "Maybe it'll bring you better luck than it did me!"

The night wore on, thick with music, laughter, and revelry. The party pulsed with spectral energy, but Ella's own had begun to fade. She leaned wearily against the crumbling mausoleum, trying to perk herself up when Able and Elizabeth appeared beside her. The shadows of dawn crept along the grave markers, but the spirits showed no sign of slowing.

Ella studied the pair through glazed-over eyes, heavy with exhaustion.

"Why are you all here?" she asked, her voice soft and unsteady. "How is this even possible? Is it... really a curse?"

Able chuckled, a low, guttural sound that curled in the air like mist. "The old curse? The one folks say 'the witch' put on this land?"

Ella blinked. "So, it's true?"

Able grinned and opened his palms wide, clearly about to launch into a tale, but Elizabeth scoffed.

"Poppycock. Just a tale we spun to scare off the living. They can't know about us, or else we lose this whole shindig, forever. Very fragile thing we've got here. No. We're here because we've found ourselves a loophole in the Ethereal Accords, and as long as we play by the rules, we get to keep this night each year."

Able scowled. "Yer a spoilsport, Lizzie."

"You're a windbag, Able, and she's tired."

He shrugged. "Fair enough."

Ella frowned. "What about me? Isn't it breaking the rules for me to be here?"

Able's grin returned, sly and almost fond. "Would've been… if you'd found us on your own. But you knocked your noggin."

"Which means, technically," said Elizabeth crisply, "You didn't find us, we found you. You weren't looking. Though in fairness, neither were we."

"Plus, you agreed t'the Ethereal Accords. See, no rules broken, assumin' that you can keep yer trap shut of course."

"Why are you being so nice to me?"

His smirk faltered. His light flickered a greenish shade of blue, and a flash of sorrow passed over his face.

"You remind me of my sister. Lilly. You're like her in a way. Sassy little minx. I miss my Lilly. I died right before she was about to get married t'that…." He stopped himself and wiped green tears away. "Oh, nuff of that," he muttered. Elizabeth patted his shoulder gently, and his smile returned a bit.

The moment was interrupted by voices calling from beyond the cemetery gates.

"Ella?" Her name rang out from beyond the gate, while

flashlights cut through the dim dawning light, distant but drawing closer. They had been so engulfed in conversation that they hadn't noticed the creeping sunrise. Around them, the spirits embraced one another in solemn farewells—kisses on cheeks, soft laughter, and goodbyes.

Elizabeth sighed, and the flames of her eyes seemed to fade a bit.

"It's time to go, Able."

She turned to Ella. "Did you enjoy your night, Ella? You certainly looked like you were having fun." Elizabeth asked with a warm smile.

Ella's face lit up. "Oh, Mrs. Sommers, it was the most fun I have ever had in my whole life." she replied with enthusiasm.

"Well," Elizabeth said, her voice fading like a soft breeze, "It was lovely to meet you, dear. I do hope to see you again."

Ella opened her mouth to respond, unsure what to say. Able took the opportunity to chime in. "So, what of it luv? See you next year? Just say, 'Sim Sala Bim!' and we'll know it's you."

"You're full of rubbish Able," said Elizabeth, vanishing like the last smoke from a cold fire.

Able just placed a finger on the side of his nose and winked at Ella.

Before she could answer, the ghosts transformed into softly shining skeletons before vanishing into puffs of smoke, blending with the morning mist. Still trying to process everything that had just happened, she was a little stunned when Nancy, Sara, and a much-abused looking Tommy arrived.

"Ella!" Nancy cried, grabbing her by the shoulders. "Thank goodness you didn't die! Are you okay?"

Nancy grabbed her shoulders, twisting her this way and that, checking for injuries. She gasped when she found the bump on Ella's head while Sara sighed, looking bored.

"I told you she'd be fine!" Sara sniffed. "You are fine, right Ella?"

Nancy would not be put off. "What happened to your head? Look at that goose egg!" she said, poking at the bump.

"Ouch." Ella swatted Nancy's hand away. "I'm okay. Honest. Just a headache…tripped and fell in the dark. I'll be fine."

Tommy narrowed his eyes, but the girls had already banded together in a tight line, marching toward the tent and chattering nonstop at Ella about waiting all night, Tommy's useless worrying, and asking questions faster than the morning mosquitoes gathered. He shook his head and went to pull the truck around.

"What happened? Everything. Tell us. Now."

What could she possibly tell them?

Ella glanced around the graveyard, remembering the ghost in the tweed with the long, long scroll. Rules. Accords. A promise. What could she tell them?

Absolutely nothing.

"Well, it started with the wind," she said, launching headlong into the longest, biggest, simplest lie of her life. Spooky sounds. A bump on the head. A night in the tent. Nancy gasped at all the appropriate places, and Sara nodded sagely as Ella described the cold and the long hours of the night. Ella worried that the story wouldn't be enough to satisfy Sara, but it was enough to do the trick—she had walked into the graveyard as an outsider. She walked out of the graveyard a legend.

"So, what do you want to do next Halloween?" Sara asked, the hint of a challenge in her voice.

"SLEEP!" cried Ella, and the three girls laughed.

She looked back as they left the gate, almost hoping to see a shadow of Able or Elizabeth. It had been one of the best nights of her life.

#   #   #

Nothing in the months that followed could match the thrill of that night. Not her fourteenth birthday, not summer vacation. not a trip to Raleigh to see a baseball game. Even cementing her place in the group of three friends, her original purpose for the graveyard trip, seemed childish and silly next to what she had witnessed. It wasn't just that ghosts were real…it was that they were also her friends.

The school year went by, but her heart remained tangled in the web of ghostly laughter and moonlit waltzes. Previously a middling student at best, Ella became the most focused student in her social studies class. The library bookshelves were suddenly bare of anything having to do with local lore, legends, history and superstition. She became obsessed with Harrington Cemetery and its residents; the ghosts' names became breadcrumbs she followed into the past.

Elizabeth Sommers (1909–1938). Second-grade teacher. Died of tuberculosis after refusing to abandon her sick students. No family, no children. Buried alone.

Dr. Harold Halverd (1885–1954). Respected town physician and councilman. Namesake of Halverd Park and the bronze statue in front of the town hospital.

Weatherington Law Offices—established 1908. "We don't just prosecute the law, we're family!"

For a little while she worried that Nancy and Sara would start asking pointed questions, but when she told them that her Halloween adventure had inspired her history paper, they shrugged and helped her with her research. Nancy was actually the best at tracking down old newspaper reports, but Sara found the jackpot in the rare books room when she found the wedding photo of Stuckley the Cowboy.

"Y'okay?" asked Sara, as Ella stared at the picture. "Y'look like ya saw a ghost."

She frantically searched for Able but struggled to find anything due to lack of records; at least, nothing local anyway. She quickly realized she did not even know his last name. She only had the name of his sister, Lilly. But even with that, nothing. A dead end.

She got an A+ on her paper and was invited to give a presentation to the local historical society. Nancy and Sara attended, uncomfortable in their fancy polyester dresses. Ella was thrilled…but nowhere near done.

\#   \#   \#

She enters the cemetery, blanketed in a thick fog, excited to see her friends. She closes the gate behind her and turns around to see only the green-glowing soldier standing in the back, eyes fixed on her, staring, expressionless. She freezes with fear when their eyes meet. His lips part as he starts to smile, but the smile is wrong. She strains to see more clearly, trying to figure out the source of her dread. His eyes glow such a bright yellow that they cast long blazes of light, almost cutting through the darkness like old flashlight beams.

There is no warning—his arms shoot out like spears, extending the entire span of the cemetery, grabbing her around the neck, and pulling her towards him with so much force that her feet were dragging behind her through the patchy moss and dirt. His cold fingers press on her windpipe, panic floods her mind. He draws her in close, and she can see now what's wrong with his smile; the teeth are broken, jagged and sharp as broken glass in the sill of a busted window. He pulls her close to his mangled mouth and rasps into her ear, "Do you see me now? Do you see me now?"

She can't scream, his fingers too tight around her neck. A wheeze like an ancient cough escapes her burning throat as he drops her to the ground. She looks back up at him. He is crying tears of blood. He covers his eyes with shaking hands and whispers, "Help me!"

She wakes up. Her throat hurts too much to scream. It takes a solid minute to fluff the marks of her terrified fingers out of her pillow. She hates that dream. She has it every week. It never changes.

\#   \#   \#

As long as the school year had been, the summer seemed even longer. Heat and time danced their slow lazy waltz across June and July and swooned into a mean yellow August. Nancy and Sara's interest in the cemetery had long since faded, and Ella did her best to keep her personal obsession to herself. At least, she thought she was doing a pretty good job. But something about the way Sara looked at her sometimes didn't feel…settled.

Nancy kicked her feet and sent ripples of light scattering across the surface of the pool. Sara lounged in a pair of Daisy Dukes and something that passed for a bikini top if you were having a real clothing emergency, while Ella floated dreamily in the middle of the pool. It was only 9:30 AM, but already the heat was climbing, and the relief of the pool would have to give way soon to the cool shade and patchy AC of Nancy's downstairs living room.

"So," said Sara, in voice heavy and thick with sweat. "What are we going to do for Halloween this year?"

Ella's instinct was to sit up in panic— an instinct that had forgotten she was floating in a swimming pool. She spluttered and coughed, pool water burning in her nose. The other girls laughed as she tried to shake water out of her eyes.

"Wh-what?"

"Th'hell is your problem?" chuckled Sara, grabbing a towel off the hot concrete. "All I asked was what we were doin' 'bout Halloween."

"There was a horsefly on me," Ella said lamely, trying to think of an excuse as she treaded water. The answer didn't seem to land.

Nancy stretched like a cat on her pool float. "I'm going to my cousins up in Shreveport. They're havin' a Halloween weddin'. You gals wanna come?"

"Hell yes, that sounds awesome! Ella, you in?"

"I'll have to see what my dad says."

But she knew what her dad would say. He would say whatever she told the girls he had said. Ella already had plans.

#   #   #

The summer rushed by like strong rapids in an angry river. However, as Halloween started to draw nearer, that speedometer slowed to a crawl. Six weeks dragged like eternity. The anticipation and nerves swelled like a tsunami of uncertainty. Nancy and Sara were wrapped up in their costumes and hairstyles for the Halloween wedding, while Ella tried to keep up the facade of disappointment, but underneath it all her emotions swallowed each other up in a storm of fears.

What if they don't show up? What if they were never real? What if I dreamt it all? What if I mess up the words? Are they going to remember me? Will Able remember me? Elizabeth? The questions were endless, limitless, and relentless.

Nancy blew her a kiss from the back seat of the truck, while Sara chucked her canvas tote with the purple stars into the back.

"Promise y'won't have any fun while we're gone, y'hear?"

Ella smiled despite herself. "Not even a little bit. Promise to have a miserable time at the coolest wedding in the entire world?"

"Total snore. Got all the movies we left ya?"

Ella held up a plastic shopping bag, ready to burst with VHS tapes.

"Start with Akira."

"Akira?"

"'s animated, you'll like it," said Sara, with a grin that Ella had learned not to trust. "Y'know, like Disney stuff."

With a whistle and a cloud of dust, Sara and Nancy were gone.

Ella sighed. She had a long, long bike ride ahead of her.

The bike basket and panniers were full to bursting. She had probably overpacked, all things considered—a lantern, a journal, a ball gown she had bought as a Halloween costume, today's newspaper, two books she had…borrowed…from the historical society, snacks, and bug spray practically spilled out into the roadway. It took her a minute to figure out the balance of the bike, but eventually she was off. According to her calculations, it should take her forty-five minutes to bike the distance.

It took two hours.

Panic that she would miss any of the party made her pump her aching legs well past the point at which she should have stopped, but as she made the trek back to the rustic wrought iron cemetery fence of Harrington Cemetery, she regretted none of it. She paused before the cemetery gates, heart pounding, and let out a huge sigh before opening them.

A full moon illuminated the headstones, brighter than she remembered the previous year. Eerie fog that seemed to only loom over this section of the hallowed grounds twisted past her feet, into the heavy stillness of the graveyard. There was nobody around, no people, no spirits, just the grass and the moss and the odd mosquito. She felt a trickle of fear slither into her heart. All she could hear were the creaking of nearby trees swaying in the wind and an owl in the distance, making the horror movie atmosphere complete. There was nothing here, but there was also nothing to lose. She took a deep breath.

"Sim Sala Bim!"

Nothing.

"Sim Sala Bim!" she cried.

Still silence. Her heart sank. She ran from grave to grave, knocking on headstones, pleading. "Please wake up! It's me, Ella!" She started running around knocking on tombstones as if they were front doors to houses. She searched desperately for Able's grave, but tears started to get in the way of her vision. How long had it been? Two minutes? Ten? Despite her best efforts, there was no answer. Crestfallen, she turned toward the exit. It had been a dream. The strangest, loveliest, most haunting of dreams. But now it was time to wake up.

"'Allo Luv. Leaving so soon? But the party hasn't begun yet."

She swung around and there they were. Able, Elizabeth, and a host of blue spirits, emerging gracefully from the mist like royalty. Her heart soared. She laughed and ran to them, embracing Elizabeth first.

"Well, hello Ella. It is lovely to see you again too dear." Elizabeth said with a chuckle.

She then lunged towards Able. With his arms open wide, she leapt into them, and he swept her into the air twirling as they ascended.

"Don't worry, luv," he whispered "I gotcha."

They floated above the graves before landing gently among the revelers. A small cheer went up from the assembly, before the party rolled into full swing—compliments of the same ghostly band. Stuckley and the cowboys were playing poker, while Elizabeth and Able joined the other couples dancing and jumping off tombstones. Everything glowed and floated about just as before, but this time Ella had brought her own party provisions. A few spectres gathered around in curious wonder as she opened a can of Coke and peeled the wrapper off a Twinkie. She laughed as they questioned her about the other 'modern wonders' she had brought with her. "I brought you all a present for later," she said, grinning mysteriously. She couldn't wait to see what they made of the newspaper.

At the edge of her vision the soldiers were gathered in their usual place, laughing and smoking just like last time. Apart and alone stood the green soldier; still facing away from the crowd and hunched over. She noticed his shoulders rising and falling in an almost rhythmic motion. Was he crying? Ella couldn't look away until Able pulled her back.

"Oi! Dance with me, will ya?"

She grinned. "I'd love to."

As the night progressed, she became more interested in getting to know more of the party's attendants. She conversed with many more ghosts this time, jotting down their names and stories in her journal to be researched later. The longest conversation of the evening, outside of Able and Elizabeth, was with the burning woman. Her name was Annalee Morgan, and she was burned at the stake for witchcraft back in 1853.

"But American witches weren't burned, they were hung. At least, that's what we learned about the Salem Witch trials."

The flaming woman laughed. "Child, do I look like someone you would meet in one of your school textbooks? How many women like me do you think never made it to the history books, or even our own local newspaper? No girl, deaths like mine are secrets. That's why I choose to keep my flames."

Annalee extended a hand, watching the blue flames lick over and under her translucent arm. "I will burn forever, and light the way for those who come after. Souls of my murderers be damned."

"What did they burn you for?"

"Witchcraft."

Ella shook her head "But what was the real reason?"

Annalee smiled, and the flames of her eyes outshone the rest. "Because I'm a witch."

The more Ella learned, the more interested she became. But her eyes and attention kept creeping back to the lonely soldier. She hated it as much as she was helpless to stop it—something about him drew her attention.

Then, on what might have been the seventeenth time she gazed over at him, he was facing her, eyes locked on her face. Suddenly, there was no one else but the two of them locked in an unbreakable stare.

"It's you." He said from across the cemetery, but she heard it as though he was sitting directly in front of her. His jaw locked in a determined scowl. He stood up and started on a course straight to her.

"It's you."

Unsure who he was talking to, she started to look around, confused; looking for anybody he could be addressing. It couldn't be her. She had never met him before.

He moved faster, other ghosts clearing a path for him. The music died as Annalee stood, pulling Ella behind her. The green soldier pointed at Ella, the line of his arm an accusation.

"You're the one!"

He kept approaching, floating towards them, almost like the wind himself. Annalee held up her right palm defensively, and Ella wondered if maybe she hadn't been joking about being a witch.

Able popped up, arms crossed over his long duster, a firm but friendly look on his kindly face.

"Easy, easy, Thomas. We wouldn't want to scare off the lil lass for good now, eh?" Able said, placing his hands on Thomas's chest to hold him back. He leaned into Thomas's ear and whispered something incomprehensible. The soldier stopped and looked up at Ella. He forced a smile that looked like he had forgotten how to, then floated back to his corner.

"Sorry about that luv." Able said to comfort Ella. "As I said, stay away from the green ones. Very unstable. And thank you Annalee for looking out for her."

"I like this one!" Annalee declared looking at Ella with approval.

"Who is that?" Ella inquired.

"His name is Thomas Elbert—he were a soldier in the Civil War fighting for the North." Able replied. "Something happened during the war that turned him dark, but 'e wont' talk about it. Ah well. He's nothing to fuss about. Carry on then." Able disappeared in a blue flash. Ella shrugged and continued to enjoy the jamboree. But she couldn't help but notice that Thomas never turned his back on the party again.

After a few rounds of poker with Stuckley and the cowboys, Ella took to exploring new areas of the graveyard. She was reading tombstones and looking for more people to converse with when she stumbled upon two ghosts locked in an embrace. It looked like one was biting the neck of the other. Ella was taken back when Elizabeth appeared out of thin air.

"Alright you two. Get a room. We have a 14-year-old present. Let's be appropriate now." Elizabeth said, raising an eyebrow that would have shot ice into the heart of any misbehaving student.

"Sorry Ella, sorry Elizabeth," the spooks muttered as they disappeared through the wall and into the mausoleum that they were leaning on. The female ghost's giggle echoed inside of the stone walls.

"Gross. What were they dooooo…" Ella's question was cut off by Elizabeth tugging her arm, dragging her back towards the party.

"I think you should show us your present, darling, dawn will be here soon you know."

Weatherton, Harold, Stuckey and a few other curious spirits gathered around. Ella presented the newspaper to the group and did her best to acquaint them with current affairs. The political stuff didn't phase them, most either not caring or noting how similar the issues were to those in their own time. The technology and science stuff however… Ella struggled to explain cell phones, CD's, video games and the AIDS epidemic. The questions flew thick and fast, but her store of knowledge was quickly depleted. She realized that she would really need to study up before the next year so she could answer the questions better. However, everyone seemed interested and grateful for the glimpse into the current world, and she promised to bring a radio with her next time.

"They still got baseball?"

"And basketball, and hockey, and—"

"The hell is basketball?"

She sighed. There was so much explaining to do.

The rest of the evening was as miraculous as the first one. That night she met so many new people it made her head swim and filled her notebook with requests for family check-ins, research, histories, and follow-ups on lost loves. Most of the haunts were kindly and respectful, but if anyone got too rowdy or too scary Able or Elizabeth always came to her rescue.

Dawn came too soon.

"G'bye lass!" said Able, giving her a hug that managed to be icy and full of warmth at the same time. "Don't grow too much!"

"The gown was perfect," said Elizabeth, "and thank you for the newspaper. It was so strange and wonderful to see how the world goes on."

"I'll have so much to tell you next time!" Ella exclaimed. She watched as they disappeared into the mist.

As exhausted as she was, she felt as though she flew home and into her bed. A whole year til the next jamboree felt like a lifetime. But the promise of a whole year to research the people and events in her notebook filled her with precious excitement.

*Annalee Morgan (1822–1853). Wife to Mayor Robert Morgan and mother of his three children. Lost to the Bayou, body never recovered. *Local Legend—reputed to be a witch, blamed for cattle disease that wiped out two herds headed west. Unclear who abducted/burned her—more research needed. NOLA library?*

Buck Nash (1873–1934). Cattle driver and town butcher. Known for his nasty reputation and his affinity for drinking and gambling. Accused of cheating and shot during a poker game.

Ashley Cripe (1882-1927). Jazz musician, bass player, and bookie. Died of natural causes. SURVIVING RELATIVE—Emily Cripe, music teacher, St. Stephen's Parish School—talk to her?

Still, Able remained a mystery. In all of the excitement, and despite all of her conversations, she had forgotten to ask him for his last name. Thomas, though, was easier to find.

Thomas Elbert (1845–1864). Son of Emery Elbert, highly respected town's blacksmith, and brother to Samuel Elbert. Both Thomas and Samuel joined the Civil War on opposing sides. On the battlefield Thomas's battalion took a stance against an advancing southern division. This initial wave of firing took a heavy toll on the south. After advancing Thomas discovered his brother shot and killed in a direct line from his personal position. He was himself killed shortly thereafter in the melee.

Thomas's story resonated with Ella. She became so fascinated with it that she deepened her research to seek any and all archives. The one that was the most helpful was the government's National Archives for Civil War Records. Upon researching the death of Samuel Elbert, she made a shocking discovery.

The Tragedy of the Elbert Twins

Thomas and Samuel Elbert were united in everything—temperament, looks, even down to the moment of their birth, the two young men walked an identical road—until the advent of the Civil War. Thomas, an avowed abolitionist, joined up with the Union army. Samuel, however, was engaged to be married to the daughter of a small but prosperous plantation owner and joined with the Confederacy. Even this division did not poison the deep well of love each twin had for the other—they often wrote letters to each other that were delivered to their mother Delilah, who then sent them on to the other's battalion.

But as fate would have it, Thomas and Samuel's outfits would meet in battle only three months into the war. During a twilight battle, Thomas's company advanced on the enemy position, where Thomas discovered his brother's body on a beeline from Thomas's previous position. According to witnesses, Thomas threw down his rifle and wept, believing that he had killed his beloved brother. He was himself killed by enemy fire within moments of dropping his weapon.

The true tragedy of the story would only be known the next morning, when army medics examining the two bodies made a staggering realization—the bullet that killed Samuel had entered his chest through the back. Samuel had been accidentally killed by friendly fire. Thomas died believing that he had killed his twin. Delilah, devastated by the news, moved her family north to Tuskaloosa. The brother's letters are currently archived in the NOLA Civil War

Reenactment Museum, which re-enacts the brothers' tragic deaths each year in honor of their story.

Friendly fire! Thomas must have been blaming himself for his brother's death for over 100 years. Emotions flooded Ella's system as she burst into tears at the thought of how much suffering Thomas had endured and for how long he had been carrying his burden. She had to tell the poor shade—the next All Hallow's Eve could not come fast enough.

The rest of the year raced by. Fourteen years turned to fifteen. Boys were on her radar now—more of her time with Sara and Nancy was spent discussing the intricacies of male politics and female posturing. Their sleepovers centered more around the web of social connections than their previously beloved horror movies. Her popularity grew in school as she gained a reputation for helping people with their history assignments. All the usual complexities of being a fifteen-year-old girl were there, but buried beneath it all was her delicious secret—her once-a-year dance with the dead in Harrington Cemetery.

"So y'all are comin', right?" drawled Sara, doodling on her math homework instead of finding Cartesian coordinates.

"Wouldn't miss it. Gary Gage is going to be there," said Nancy, a little breathless. Gary Gage and his grey eyes were almost all she talked about.

"Coming to what?" Ella asked, setting down her backpack. Nancy scooted her English notebook over to make room.

"The Halloween dance. St. Stephens is throwin' one in the

basement, said they're tryin' ta keep us rep-ro-bates off the streets and doin' some wholesome dancin'."

Even Nancy snorted at that. "They haven't seen the way y'all dance."

Ella started to shake her head, but Sara's stare stopped her. "Don't tell me you're skippin' out on this one too?"

"N-no..." Ella stammered, feeling trapped. She had forgotten to come up with a good excuse for missing this Halloween. "Of course I'm coming. But how late does it go? My curfew is 9:30."

"Come on Ella, your dad can't be that strict on Halloween. Want my parents to talk to him?"

"Thanks Nance. Let me talk to him about it, I'll see what he says first."

Sara clapped her hands "Perfect! We're goin' as Josie and the Pussycats."

"You just want to wear your sister's leg warmers."

"Do not."

Ella sighed as her friends bantered. How was she getting out of this one?

In the end, her plan felt like something out of a spy novel. She spent the days leading up to the dance sneaking pepper into her hand and faking sneezes, hiding ice packs in her backpack to make her hands and forehead clammy, and generally faking the best cold she could. At home, she talked up what a wonderful time she was going to have at the dance, and not to expect her until the next morning. The news was met with her father's typical dismissive wave as he buried himself in another set of slides and peer reviewed articles.

Though she hated to sacrifice time on Halloween, she did her best to balance her friends and her secret. She pretended to feel sick at the dance, and by 10:45 (after three dances with her friends and one with a cute but not terribly interesting boy from the next town over) she was in a cab headed toward the Jamboree.

By the time her boots touched the mossy paths of Harrington Cemetery, the party was already in full swing.

Music swirled through the trees—sweet, ghostly jazz with a New Orleans soul. The kind of music that made even the tombstones sway. Candles floated like fireflies above the graves, and laughter— thin and echoing—spilled through the air like perfume from another time. The living would have been terrified. But Ella felt only joy.

She broke into a run, darting between polished headstones in the newer part of the cemetery. Her heartbeat with the rhythm of the music, her breath catching in the still air. As she rounded the final bend, two familiar figures appeared at the iron gates: Able, dapper as ever in his old-time English suit, and Elizabeth, with her lavalier drifting in the wind like smoke.

"'Allo, luv," Able called out with a grin. "Knew you'd make it. Though you kept us holdin' our breath, didn't ya?" He winked. "A wee bit late, eh?"

Ella laughed breathlessly, throwing herself into their waiting arms. Their touch was like cold sparks—but warm in its own way. A reunion of souls, living and not. But this time, she wasn't just here for the party. She had a purpose.

Ella pulled away, her chest tight with resolve. There was something crawling under her skin— an array of fear, urgency, and determination all tightly woven into a thick braid. Her hand clutched the folder tucked inside her coat. She looked across the graveyard and spotted him; Thomas, hunched at the edge of the old chapel ruins, cradled in sorrow like a burden he couldn't let go.

Last year, he'd terrified her. His grief was heavy and wild, swirling around him like a storm. But this year, Ella knew something he didn't—his suffering might have an end. She had found the truth.

She walked towards him, but before she could take more than a few strides, Able was suddenly in front of her, blocking her path with gentle firmness. His eyes were no longer smiling.

"Ella, dear... let's just leave that one be, eh?" he said quietly. "Nuffin' good ever comes from stirrin' his pain."

"No, Able," she said, steady but pleading. "I found something. Something that might give him peace. But please… stay close. Just in case."

Able hesitated, his pale flame eyes full of concern. Then he gave a reluctant nod. "Alright, luv. But I don't like it."

Ella moved forward alone, her steps soft but sure. As she approached, Thomas sat motionless, his shoulders trembling with quiet sobs. He didn't seem to notice her—until she reached out and laid a hand gently on his back.

A spark passed between them—cold, electric, almost like static from a forgotten dream.

"Thomas?" she said softly.

His head lifted. His face was pale and hollow, eyes wide with sorrow, but something in them flickered when he saw her.

"Oh," he murmured. "It's you."

"I'm Ella," she said. "I have something that I need to tell you…It's about your brother." The light in his eyes vanished like flames snuffed by the wind.

Ella didn't hesitate. She knelt beside him, opening the folder. She laid out documents with trembling fingers, reading through the old report that told the truth—Sam's death was an accident and caused by friendly fire, not the betrayal Thomas had been burdened with for so long. She told him everything, her voice steady, the wind catching her words and carrying them through the crypts. When she finished, silence blanketed the graveyard. Thomas stared out beyond the gates, expressionless. For a moment, Ella feared she'd lost him.

And then—he broke. Not in rage, not in terror—but in tears. A deep, wrenching sob that seemed to shake the soil. Ella looked back at Able, confused, frightened. Able only shrugged, equally unsure. Then she noticed something strange—Thomas' tears were shining. Soft blue trails ran down his cheeks, washing away the green, tears of sorrow and release. The same radiant hue the others wore when they'd found peace.

Thomas stood, slowly, straightening for the first time since she had met him. His face, streaked with glowing tears, looked younger, stronger. Beautiful in a way that hurt to see, yet she couldn't look away. He was breathtaking, and she was noticing it for the first time.

"My dear brother… I am so sorry. You told me to never despair, but that is exactly what I did. I fell into despair. Now we are both in the beyond. Please forgive me. I love you, Sam," he whispered to the stars.

He turned to Ella, his blue-lit face full of gratitude.

"I knew it was you," he said, voice shaking. "I dreamt of you. I dreamt of someone who would set me free. End my misery. I just didn't know how… not until now. Thank you, Ella," he said, his voice full of something deep and real. "I don't know how to repay you." Then, turning to the party behind them, he cried out, voice echoing like thunder through the stones. "I didn't kill my brother!"

The music stopped. For a moment, silence reigned. Then, like a wave breaking, the ghosts cheered. A hundred voices lifted in celebration—of truth, of healing, of redemption. Light burst around them, glowing blue and gold, drifting like lanterns into the sky.

"Oi!" Able laughed from the gates, tears of his own in his eyes, remembering his own sibling. "Looks like we've got one more joinin' the party!"

Thomas slowly levitated over to his fellow soldiers, as they welcomed him with pats on his back, while another one handed him a cigar and lit it with a blue flame that sprouted from the tip of his index finger. The music kicked back up and the party recommenced, but her heart was full.

Able looked over at Ella with a look of so much pride that she could feel it emanating from him like a warm flame on a cold night.

"Unbelievable, luv. Come ear, would ya?" He called her over to stand right next to him. Able took his index finger and swiped it on the back of his own fist. He then grabbed her hand. "Make a fist, darling." He ordered. She complied. He drew a heart shape on the back of her fist with what looked like ash. The black heart shape was a symbol.

"Here you are, luv. It's a heart… because that's what you

are. You're all heart." She looked down at the symbol, her breath catching. It felt like something holy—fragile and timeless. For a moment, she imagined it etching into her soul like a mark of belonging. She clasped her wrist, eyes not leaving the black heart. She knew it would fade with the dawn, but part of her knew it wouldn't.

As the night neared its end, but still with enough time, Thomas snuck over to Ella. He tapped on her shoulder and leaned in. "May I have this dance, Ella?" he asked, bowing low, palm extended like a knight from a war-torn fairytale. Her cheeks flushed, but before she answered, she met eyes with Elizabeth. She looked at Elizabeth as if to say, What should I do? Elizabeth just smiled slightly and tilted her head as if to say, *why not?*

Ella smiled and took his hand, and they danced till the sun came up. They moved together through the mist and music, spinning between the headstones and ancient oaks. Their dance was weightless yet grounded in something deeper. They spoke of childhood memories, of courage and sacrifice, of dreams they barely understood. She didn't want it to end, but the first blush of sunlight began to chase the shadows from the cemetery. As the fog started to pull back like a curtain at the end of a play, he spoke.

"Thank you again, sweet Ella, for everything. I could never repay you." He took her hand, once again bowed, and kissed her hand ever so gently. She felt the sparks once again from the physical connection, only now she felt sparks everywhere. She wondered if this is what people meant when they said they 'lit up like a Christmas tree'. Just then he smiled as he faded into the morning dew. With her hand in place from where he kissed her, she glanced at the ash heart still on her hand and realized she was alone again.

\#   \#   \#

"Ella? Ella. ELLA."

"Hmm? What?"

"Snap out of it, or you can study for the geometry exam by yourself. It's like talking to a wall with you lately!"

"Sorry Nance," Ella mumbled, and shook her head as though she could shake off the exhaustion.

"Y'stayed up all night again, din'ya?"

Sara was smirking at her again. Ella hated to give her the satisfaction.

"Just bad dreams, that's all. Okay, PEMDAS, let's go."

Nancy shook her own head at the two of them, clearly fed up. "PEMDAS is Algebra, you need the formulas for area. I swear, you two need the Pythagorean Theorem like some folks need religion."

"Maybe that's what her bad dreams are 'bout," Sara snarked. Ella shot her a glance and sighed. Sara wasn't convinced.

And she was right not to be. Ella hadn't had a nightmare in months. Now, she often relived the final hours of the last party, dancing and whispering with Thomas. It was often Thomas that she would wake up thinking about. On occasion, in her dreams, his final kiss found its way to her lips. From those, she would wake up bemused. *What is wrong with me?*

Nothing. Just dreams, they meant nothing. Dreams were just brain ghosts you saw in your sleep.

Ghosts.

She picked up her pencil, gritting her teeth, ready for fractions or volume or whatever it was that Nancy was chattering about.

"Right. Okay. Area of a circle."

"Damnit Ella will y' just tell us his name already?"

Nancy was about to burst. *"Pythagoras, Sara!"*

"No dummy, the boy she's in love with."

"I'm not in love."

Both girls turned to her, and she felt pinned like a butterfly on display by their stares.

"You're tired all the time, you daydream constantly, you barely eat, and you spend all your time writing in those journals of yours," said Nancy in a voice so tart that it could sour milk at fifty paces. "Your grades are slipping, and you've started wearing makeup on weekdays. A squared plus B squared equals C squared."

"So, what's his name?"

Ella could feel her molars grinding. They had her dead to rights. She flipped through the rolodex in her head of boys they knew, boys in their class, boys in the class ahead of them. It wouldn't work. They would go straight to any of those boys and hound them about her. She would have to tell them the truth—at least enough of it to get them off her back.

"He's…older. You won't know him."

Sara's gaze became pinpoints of accusation; Ella could feel them boring into her brain.

"Try us."

Here it was. No going back.

"Thomas."

Nancy and Sara sat back in their seats as though they had been slapped. Ella blinked, surprised. Was there someone in their class named Thomas she had forgotten about? Why were they so shocked?

"T-tommy?" spat Sara, wild eyed.

"Her *brother?!*" gasped Nancy.

Oh shit.

Wait.

PERFECT.

"I... I didn't want to tell you. I thought it would get weird."
Sara snapped her textbook shut.

"Y'damn right it's weird. Too weird. That's just gross Ella. "

"Sara, I just—"

"Y'all have a crush on my brother, an' you think you can sit an' study like it ain't nothin?"

Nancy shifted uncomfortably. "Sara, come on, I think you're—"

"Think I'm what? Friends do NOT date friends' kin. Plus, Tommy is four years older than us, it's disgusting."

"No one said anything about dating him Sara," Ella snapped. Her cheeks were flushed—this ploy was working just a little too well. She hadn't expected Sara to get this upset.

"Well good, because it ain't happenin'. Just like this study session."

With a swish of jean skirt and a toss of wild curls, Sara was gone. Nancy glanced at Ella apologetically.

"She'll calm down after a bit. We had another friend, Louisa Jean, who dated Tommy for a while. It didn't go well, and…well, she still has her brother, but we don't have Louisa Jean anymore. You see? She cares about you, or she wouldn't be so mad."

Nancy patted her hand and left her alone at the library table. Her secret was safe…but was her friendship? She had only taken the graveyard dare to cement her friendship with Sara and Nancy in the first place. Maybe she wasn't really spending enough time in the land of the living.

Ella stared at the pages of the geometry book, but they twisted and swam in unexpected tears. She'd been a bad friend. That needed to change. It *would* change.

After Halloween.

#   #   #

Sara did calm down…after a week or so. Ella attributed a lot of this to the fact that she, Ella, now had both a car and a driver's license, and Sara had an urge to go places. The three of them tooled around the Parish in what was admittedly a jalopy, but it was more car than most kids at school had. They were even so bold one weekend as to drive all the way up to Shreveport to go to the new mall and had the time of their lives. Ella splurged on a new makeup set, a palette of ghostly greys and blues.

"You'll look like a hooker," snorted Sara. "Or a haint."

"Mind your business," said Ella, but inwardly she smiled. She couldn't wait to see the look on Able's face when she showed up in glowing blues to match all of them.

Sara handed her a pair of blue rhinestone earrings. "Here, these'll match."

"Thanks!"

Nancy was unimpressed. "What are you going to be for Halloween, a Smurf?"

"What is it you two have against the color blue?"

They shrugged, but Nancy looked uneasy.

"Haint blue," she said finally. "It's the color that wards off death. Gives me the creeps is all."

"Speakin' of," said Sara, turning her attention to a patched leather jacket. "What're you doin for Halloween?"

"Oh, I'm…I'm…"

She hadn't prepared a lie for this year yet. Halloween was still a month away.

"Ditchin' us again?"

"No," she snapped, frustrated at herself for not being more prepared. "And when have I ever ditched on you?"

"She wasn't invited to the wedding," Nancy said gently, trying to get ahead of the brewing fight between her two friends.

"She could've come."

"I'm sorry, did I do something wrong by going home and puking my guts out because I ate bad shrimp at the dance last year?"

Sara's face darkened and she dropped the sleeve of the jacket. "No."

Ella remembered the promise to herself about being a better

friend. The thought of giving up any time at the graveyard was painful, but the idea of losing the friends that she had the other 364 days of the year…

"Listen. Let's do a movie night this year, okay? We'll rent some absolute trash movies with tons of gore, we'll eat popcorn and I dunno, do a Ouija board or something. What do you say?"

"We are NOT doing a Ouija board—" Nancy practically shrieked. "My mother will have a cow. She'll have more than a cow; she'll have a whole herd!"

Sara and Ella doubled over laughing at Nancy, earning them a steady glare from the bored college student at the checkout.

"Deal," said Sara, the light back in her eyes. "Let's get an Orange Julius for the ride home."

Ella shook off her guilt. She *would* hang out with them and watch a movie or two…until they fell asleep. Then, off to the cemetery. It would be a snap to get there now that she had a car instead of having to hoof it. Perfection.

#   #   #

It took forever for them to fall asleep.

They had watched *Terror at Camp Hatchet,* the original *and* the really quite awful sequel, eaten a kiddie pool's worth of popcorn with extra butter and salt, and the other two girls had still only fallen asleep after she pointed out that Nancy had church in the morning. It was a mad dash to throw on her full Victorian style blue gown, style her hair, and carefully apply the blue and silver makeup. By the time she finally made it to the cemetery, she was cursing the clock and racing toward the ball like a reverse Cinderella. It was already 2 AM.

She flung open the gate to a quiet and still cemetery and yelled, "Sim Sala Bim, guys. It's me Ella."

The air shifted. Cold static tickled her lips, and pressure settled across her mouth as if unseen hands cupped her face. Then Able appeared, faint and serious for once. "Shhhhh," he whispered, putting a finger to his lips. He gestured, tilting his head to throw her attention in a certain direction. He pointed to just outside of their inner gate -there were four teenagers all dressed in cloaks sitting around a grave in the newer section. They had a Ouija board and flashlights.

Ella nodded as Able disappeared. Her mind raced. She knew she had to do something or else this night would be ruined. She had to do something, but what?

She snuck back out to her car, which was parked back on the street in front of the main gates, and grabbed a flashlight. She tiptoed her way back near the group of teens, held her flashlight up to her forehead to make herself appear taller, and shined the light on the teens. "GET THEE GONE!" she boomed, deepening her voice. "THIS IS NOT THY REALM WHEN THE SUN IS DOWN!" The teens shrieked, scrambled, and scattered like frightened crows. Ella barely held in her laughter as she watched one toss a flashlight over the fence before tumbling after it.

Able manifested and smacked his hands together. "And STAY out!" he roared, grinning ear to ear. "Alright, lasses and lads, let's give three cheers for tonight's hero—Ella!" A cheer rose from the fog, as spirits flickered into being, clapping, howling, leaping in celebration. Able turned to her, eyebrows raised. "You're a clever one, ain'tcha?" She smiled, held up her fist, and thrust it forward. He blinked, then laughed a belly-deep laugh. "Right then." With a swirl of his finger across his own hand, he drew the ash heart once more on hers. She smiled and nodded. A tradition now.

"Now," he said, spreading his arms, "Let's party!" And with that, the cemetery came alive. Ghosts of every kind emerged from crypts and shadows—ladies in tattered ball gowns, sailors with seaweed still tangled in their beards, children with lanterns of bone and pumpkin. Ella wandered among them, greeted by name, embraced by the dead.

She scanned the usual mob, but something was different. She searched. There was no flicker of green in the crowd. No Thomas waiting, quiet, and apart. Had he moved on? Had she set him free? Her chest tightened with selfless hope and selfish disappointment. She made one final desperate sweep with her eyes.

There he was! He was standing still, blending in with his comrades, looking directly at her, no longer flickering green, but a brilliant, full blue. Vibrant. Peaceful. Proud. Once their eyes met, he shot her a smirk followed by a wink. Her heart fluttered, and he made his way across the green.

"Well, miss Ella. You look absolutely radiant this evening." he said, bowing and kissing her hand.

"I could say the same about you, in your dapper blue tint," she said, trying not to be breathless. Was this flirting? Her heart rate suggested it might be.

"Thanks to you."

That night, they stayed close. They laughed, told story after story, and danced again beneath the moonlight and the dying stars. The music of the dead rang through the night, and Ella felt—for a fleeting moment—that she belonged to both worlds.

They made the rounds of the party—Ella sipping a can of soda, Thomas with a glass of ghost brew—playing a game of poker with the cowboys, dancing with Able and Elizabeth, and paying their respects to Annalee, wreathed as ever in her blue flames.

But mostly what they did was talk. They talked in the way that young people do, about everything and nothing and anything in between that caught their fancy. Time didn't matter—neither the time between their beginnings and endings, or the time that was passing like sand in a glass. Everything was perfect for a short, sweet while.

But as it must, dawn crept in with quiet cruelty. The night flew by, a brittle leaf carried off by a violent wind, leaving so much unsaid between them. Their bond had blossomed with such unparalleled speed that it felt almost sacred, like a rose blooming under the frost. As that morning light grew, she found herself missing him even before he had even gone.

When it came time to say goodbye, she embraced her phantom friends with warmth—but when she reached Thomas, her arms lingered around him much longer. It was a desperate, silent plea to halt the inevitable. Thomas, too, held her tightly. Eyes shut, they pressed together in a final embrace.

Nearby, Able watched with a furrowed brow, his jovial demeanor dimmed. His gaze met Elizabeth's across the fading party, and in her silence, he saw his concern mirrored. But neither Ella nor Thomas had noticed. Their world, for that moment, contained only each other.

The sun shone through her closed eyelids and her arms folded into herself as he dissipated. He was gone. When she finally slipped back into her bed, sneaking over the snoring Sara and trying desperately not to step on Nancy's retainer case, all she could think about was the last moment she felt the cold prickle of his hands on hers.

It's all she would have for another year.

\#   \#   \#

As the calendar turned, Ella's seventeenth birthday arrived and went. Boys at school trailed behind her like moths drawn to a flame they didn't understand. But Ella barely noticed them. How could she? Her thoughts were inked with the memory of a spectral soldier whose touch still echoed within her. Thomas was a ghost, yes, but it felt as though he had etched his name onto her innermost heart. Nothing in the waking world could ever compare.

Sara and Nancy seemed none the wiser, though Sara still shot her the odd suspicious glance now and then as Ella's notebooks got thicker and thicker with notes, research, and odd newspaper scraps. This year brought more research, topped off with a haunting new discovery; she had found the parish records for the cemetery, and buried between a murdered child and a victim of the Spanish flu, she finally found Able.

Able Davies (1919– Presumption of Death 1953). Shipbuilder and iron worker. Survived by sister Lilly Davies. Disappeared from Hampshire, England in 1950. Presumed dead in 1953.

What happened to Able? And what was he doing here? Everyone else she researched was actually buried there. According to all records, Able was not. City records showed that all the other ghosts she associated with were documented, with the location of their burial sites. No sign of Able. *What did this mean?*

She remembered something Able said years ago.

I miss my Lilly. I died right before she was about to get married to that… She replayed the words in her head. She remembers the melancholy look on his face. *Who?* Ella thought. *Who was she getting married to?*

It took three weeks for the inter-library loan service to find what she was looking for, but the wait was worth it. The microfilm of the newspaper clippings was exactly what she was after. She scribbled furiously in her notebook, her heart sinking as a picture of just what had befallen her friend started to take shape.

Anderson Wells (1922– 1991). Successful businessman and commerceman. Made his fortune building Wells Shipping and Imports. Known for his strong and aggressive personality, he always had a way of getting what he wanted. Married to Lilly Davies and survived by his two children Charles Wells and Sandra Wells. Maybe Able still has a living family!

Ella dug deeper. Luckily, Anderson was not a very private

man, nor terribly discreet—his shenanigans popped up in the local newspapers quite regularly, and if her understanding of British understatement was working properly, it was clear that he was not a popular man. Gambling, drinking, assault…yet he never served any time in jail. It seemed like he was so wealthy that he was above the law. All signs pointed to the fact that he was not a good guy, at all.

She wanted to find out if there was any connection to the cemetery's location and either Able, Lilly, or Anderson. She had to find out why Able was there.

Eventually her research led to real estate: Wells Shipping and Imports owned a warehouse in Alexandria, LA, only a few miles to the south of Harrington Cemetery, Ella knew it was way too much of a coincidence. *What did you do to Able, Anderson?*

A backpack dropped onto the table beside her, and she nearly jumped out of her skin. Sara grinned, while Nancy hung back looking anxious. Well, more anxious than usual.

"Halloween Night. Shreveport. There's going to be a rave, and we are going to be there," Sara said, barely reining in her excitement.

"How? There's no way Nancy's mom—"

"Mom said I could go as long as I'm with my cousin Justice. He's going to keep an eye on me."

"To a *rave?*"

"Dance," said Nancy defensively. "We're going to a dance."

"We're going to a rave," said Sara triumphantly, and waited for Ella to light up with enthusiasm. Ella was walking right into the trap.

"We're…going to a rave!" Ella cried, hoping she was a decent actress. It seemed to have done the job.

Sara clapped her hands on the table and scooped up the backpack.

"Start planning your outfit and saving up gas money girls. It's going to be *wild.*"

She disappeared among the bookshelves, leaving Nancy and Ella to eye each other warily in her wake.

Nancy broke the silence first.

"You don't want to go."

"Neither do you," Ella levelled back at her coolly. Nancy's look of vague relief told her she had hit the target on her guess.

"No…it's not that I don't want to go…I just don't really know anyone besides Justice, and he's not really interested in…well he doesn't behave like—"

"He's not really going to be much of a babysitter?"

"…no."

Ella tented her fingers and gazed at her friend. Nancy was a walking poster child for perfectionistic anxiety, but she was also a good friend and had a level-headed demeanor that kept the peace more often than not. She reminded Ella of Elizabeth. Nancy caught a breath and then countered.

"You don't want to go either."

"Of course I do," Ella lied, trying not to look away. Stuckley had taught her that when you bluff, it's best to do it with your eyes open and on your target. "I just can't."

"Why not?"

"I have a date."

"*A DATE?!*"

"Shhh Nancy PLEASE, keep your voice down."

"With who? Where? When? Sara is going to *kill you* ohmygod don't tell me it's with Tommy."

Ella winced. She felt awful about it, but Tommy was just going to have to be collateral damage.

"I told you, it's not Tommy, but if it makes the two of you feel better thinking that it is, go right ahead. I have a date, I am not going to the rave, and honestly even if I didn't have a date after how sick I got at the dance last time I wouldn't want to go all the way to Shreveport anyway."

"So, it's a date, so what, reschedule, you can reschedule a date you can't reschedule Halloween!"

"What is so damn important about Halloween?"

"I don't know, I'm not in Sara's head! But it's important to her."

"Well, this date is important to me!"

"Well, which is more important, your friendship or your date?"

"If my friend doesn't support me enough to let me go on a date, then is it really a friendship?"

Nancy threw up her hands in exasperation. "What do you want me to do? Lie to her?"

"No, just… listen, can we compromise?"

"Define compromise."

"I'll go to the rave…but I'll leave early, we'll pretend that my dad called to yell at me because I snuck out to go to this thing. I'll go on my date and come back and pick you both up in the morning."

Nancy shook her head. "Compromise means we both get something we want. What am I getting?"

"What do you want?"

"A nice Halloween like we had last year before you snuck out."

That landed on her like a pile of bricks.

"Who snuck out?"

"You did. In your blue dress. And no, I didn't tell Sara. I can keep a secret."

Ella let out a pent-up breath in relief. "You're a good friend."

"And you aren't. Okay that was harsh…you're…not a bad friend but you're not exactly winning friend of the year."

Her cheeks burned with shame, and her gaze dropped to the floor. "Yeah. I know. I'm sorry Nancy."

The other girl's stance softened, and she shrugged. "It's okay. It's not like you've had great examples to copy from. But you have to tell us what this is about sooner or later. You *have* to."

"I… Nancy I can't. I really can't. If I break the rules—"

"What rules?"

"Gaaah Nancy I can't tell you! I'm not even sure if I broke the rules by telling you that there are rules!"

"What happens if you break them?"

"I don't know! But nothing good!"

Nancy stared at her, and Ella realized that her voice had risen to a fever pitch. She clapped a hand over her mouth and tried to get herself back under control.

"Ella…are you in trouble? Like… in a cult, or something?"

She shook her head at Nancy's question. But something had started to unravel. She wasn't sure anymore that she could stop it.

"No, no, nothing like that, I just… I just can't. Please."

There was a gentle pressure on her shoulder, and she looked up. Nancy was watching her with genuine worry etched on her sweet, freckled face.

"It's okay. Whatever it is…I'm here for you, okay? We both are."

Ella nodded silently, tears rolling down her face. She was a bad friend. And here was Nancy, a warm hand on her shoulder. Real. All year. Every year.

But she wasn't Thomas.

"I'll…we'll figure it out with Sara, okay?"

Ella nodded.

Behind the bookcases, Sara smiled.

#   #   #

A simple plan is always the best plan.

This was not the best plan, but it was the one they had.

Just getting ready had taken them three hours. Zephyrs of perfume and clouds of hairspray followed them into the car and would have choked them if not for the rolled down windows and cool evening breeze. They would go to the rave, Ella would get a 'phone call' from her dad telling her that she had to come home immediately, leaving Nancy and Sara to squeeze into the truck with Tommy to get home the next morning. Ella would drive off and make it to the cemetery by midnight. It was all arranged.

The silver lining to her plan was that Tommy was officially off the suspect list of boys she was dating, so Sara had at least stopped being suspicious about that. In fact, the closer they had gotten to Halloween, the happier and…well…better things had been between them. Things between Nancy and Ella, however, had gotten more tense. She almost couldn't wait for the night to be over and for things to get back to 'normal'.

Almost.

"11:00. Let's get crazy girls!" Sara practically dove onto the dance floor, leaving Ella and Nancy to navigate their way through a swirling morass of bodies, sweat, and adolescent nerves.

"You good?" Nancy shouted above the din.

"Yeah. I'll see you Monday. And Nancy? Thanks."

Nancy nodded and followed Sara into the crowd. Ella waved at them, pretending to dance, but watching the clock the whole time. 11:15. 11:20. 11:30.

Ella slipped out, Cinderella like, into the car and away into the night.

#　　#　　#

Normally she enjoyed the walk to the old cemetery, but tonight she ran-the need to see Thomas was so compelling, she could almost feel him pulling her.

"Sim Sala Bim!"

She balled her fist and shoved it in front of her. A deep chuckle resonated and rolled through the empty headstones and obelisks, as the ceremonial black ash heart appeared on her skin. Her giggle added to the chuckle as everyone flashed into vision in puffs of smoke. With no further adieu, the jamboree was underway.

The reunion with Able and Elizabeth was warm, however, there was no sign of Thomas. Her eyes scrambled through the sea of glowing blue.

"Is he here?"

"Not yet, he was finishing something up on the Other. I'm sure you'll see him soon," said Elizabeth, smiling. "And I'm sure he'll be as glad to see you as you are to see him. Just…don't get too wrapped up in it, all right? A flirtation is a lovely thing, but that's all it should be darling."

Ella frowned but was soon distracted by Able pulling her into a rollicking jig. She was here; it was enough.

Ghostly fireflies danced in the shadows, adding a flickering, magical ambiance as the sharp high tones of trumpets and trombones ricocheted off of stone and marble slabs. Floating hands held candles and bottles of Sanguis Mortuus as the contagion of jollity consumed every spirit in Harrington, the living and the dead.

Ella didn't waste any time. "Able? I have a… weird question to ask you. I don't want to upset you, I—"

"I'm dead darlin', what could upset me? Shoot, luv."

"Who is Anderson Wells?"

Able froze, shocked, but tried to shake it off. He pulled Ella out of the dance and over to a small tree.

"He's a bloody tosser! 'ow do you know 'is name?"

"I looked into your family's history in hopes of finding out why you don't have a tombstone, I—"

"He is a bad, bad man. He treats people like rubbish an' he's a bloody criminal. Real scum. Last I heard, Lilly was set to marry 'im. I wasn't havin' it. I told 'im he wasn't good enough for my sweet Lilly."

Able was pacing now, clenching and unclenching his hands. Ella was starting to worry.

"If he was so bad, why was Lilly going to marry him?"

"Well, he was young, 'andsom, and wealthy. He dazzled her with gifts, big showy declarations of love, all that dross. She was smitten. He wanted her because she was everything he couldn't buy outright—a soul as beautiful as the sun on a spring day."

"Yeah, we call that love bombing these days. Sounds like a real creep."

"I raised 'er since she was eight." Tears welled in his eyes. "He didn't even ask for me blessin. Last time I talked to him, I told him that there was no way I'd let him marry her. He told me it didn't matter what I thought. He was gonna marry her anyway. I told him, 'Over my' dead body'. Next thing I know I'm 'ere, with these fine folks.'

"Able I think…I think he killed you to get to Lilly, then secretly shipped your body and buried you here in an unmarked grave."

They stood in silence for a while, one breathing, one not.

"Suppose that would answer why I'm 'ere, instead of buried next to me mum. What scum, eh?" After a moment of consideration, his face straightened. "What became of 'er, my Lilly?"

"Well, they did get married, and she lived to sixty-nine years old. Had two children."

"Ay, I'm an uncle."

"And a great uncle," Ella said with a smile.

"How'd she die?" he asked, trying to mask the sadness mixed in with his curiosity. .

"She had a heart attack. She had one prior, but it was the second that took her."

"So, it wasn't' im?"

She shook her head, not sure if that made him feel better or not.

"Thank you, luv. I've been worrying about her for over forty years. It puts my heart to rest like nothin' else could have."

Ella wrapped her arms around him and squeezed Able around his chest, as his emotions ran over her like rain. It felt like his whole ghostly form would shake into nothingness if she didn't hold on to him tightly. After a minute, he wiped the blue flames of his eyes.

"S'all right. Come on luv, we've got partying to do."

#   #   #

"Let's go, party's over."

"Wait, *what?* Sara! Stop!"

Sara had Nancy by the wrist and was dragging her at a sharp pace toward the door. Nancy knew from their childhood bouts of roughhousing that she was better off just going along rather than trying to pull away when Sara had that death grip.

"Why are we leaving? We *just got here.*"

Sara turned abruptly, and Nancy nearly crashed into her. Chest to chest, Sara's eyes glared into her friend's, a wild light behind them.

This was not going according to plan.

"Because Ella's leaving. And we're goin't follow her."

"Sh-she is?"

Sara rolled her eyes "Stop pretendin' you don't know. Stop pretendin' you don't notice how she's been acting weirder and weirder every year. Stop pretendin' you haven't realized that she disappears *every Halloween.* Or am I the only one worried about her? She's in a cult or somethin' Nancy; it's the only explanation for all her weird journals and notes and stuff. Something is *wrong*, and I'm not goin' ta let it go until I know *why*."

"But—"

"*She's our friend*, Nancy."

Nancy's mouth closed, and her jaw set guiltily. Sara nodded slowly.

"You already knew she was gonna leave."

"She said there were rules, and if she broke them something bad would happen. I think you might be right that it's a cult or something."

"Then shut up and hoof it heifer, before she makes it out of the parking lot and we lose her. You can tell me the rest while we drive."

Tommy didn't discover that his truck had been hijacked for several hours. By then, it was far too late.

#   #   #

Able and Ella turned back to the revel and were ready to step back onto the dance floor, when a glimmer of movement caught her eye. They both turned toward a small mausoleum on the right.

Her breath was taken when she saw Thomas walk out through a closed mausoleum door, wearing the tattered remnants of what had been a very fancy suit. Her heart fluttered like hummingbird wings as he approached. He looked like a literal angel; perfect face, dressed to the nines, grinning with so much panache that she nearly melted where she stood.

"There's my lady," he said, making a slow beeline for her.

"Say that again," Ella whispered, barely audible over the music.

"There's my lady," he said again, holding out his hand.

"Yeah." She smiled wider than her face could afford. "I like that."

"As always, you look absolutely breathtaking. Well, if I had a breath to take."

"And you. Wow. You look… I didn't know you could change your clothes." Ella said, examining the outfit.

"You can't. I mean, unless they bury you with a change

of clothes. Which they don't. Damn, I'm babbling like a fool, my apologies—"

"But—"

Elizabeth joined them and started laughing as Mr. Weatherton stumbled out of the same mausoleum that Thomas had come out of. He was fixing his belt, and wearing a tattered Civil War soldier's uniform, with a badge that said T. Elbert. He then looked up at his admirers with a very disapproving look.

"Oh, I see." Ella said, fighting back laughter. "Well, thank you for helping Thomas, sir."

"I did not do it for him!" Weatherton spat, trying to maintain his distinguished posture and adjusting his top hat—the only original article of clothing he still wore from his own.

"Well, then I thank you." She said giving a slight curtsey. "You know, you would have made a mighty fine soldier, Mr. Weatherton." Laughter erupted between Ella, Thomas, Able and Elizabeth. Weatherton harrumphed and moseyed off to enjoy a drink.

"Well, milady." Thomas said as he bowed and held out his hand.

Reaching to take his hand, she felt a zap. Much stronger than the normal buzz whenever she touched another ghost; this actually felt like a jolt of electricity. She reached again and grabbed it this time. Suddenly, there was no blueish tint where their two hands touched, instead, a light pink color radiated. More mesmerized than shocked, he quickly kissed her hand and let go. Luckily, the party was in full swing, so the flash of color hadn't disturbed the other spirits.

However, Elizabeth and Able witnessed the change. They exchanged concerned glances.

"Able, what was that? Why did it glow pink?" Ella asked.

"No bloomin 'idea, luv. I've only seen it...."

"Love!" Elizabeth interjected. "It's love."

Ella blushed and started to squirm under the scrutiny of the spirits. Able was clearly upset and Elizabeth was not far behind him.

Thomas held his head up proudly. "It's true. I am not afraid to say it."

Able shook his head darkly. "You should be mate. We've got ourselves a little problem. You've done broke Ethereal Accords rule number six. You've gone and' fallen for each other. Now, I'm not one to play dad on ya, but for the best interest of everyone, you two can only be friends. You've got t'shut this down, *now*. D'you understand?"

Ella could feel the heartbreak starting at the top and radiating downward through her chest. She could see it echoing in Able's face.

Thomas grasped her hand tightly, the pink flare brightening closer to red. It scared Ella a bit. "I contest! Why? Why is love in any capacity wrong?"

Elizabeth stepped closer, as though she were trying to get close to a dangerous fire without getting burned.

"Because you are dead, Thomas, and she is not. Nobody is saying it is wrong because of social reasons, it's wrong because of the consequences it will have on the veil of the living and the dead and the unraveling of the very fabric of both realities. You must understand, this is quite serious."

Elizabeth licked her lips, looking more and more panicked as

Thomas and Ella stood silent.

"Serious beyond the stakes of life and death darlings, as serious as eternity. You *must* let go of each other, right *now.*"

Thomas stood ramrod straight, and the red started spreading up his body. Ella stared, then turned to Able, fear starting to clear her head when Thomas spoke again.

"My heart knows what it wants. My love is not something that can be turned off and on like a switch." He stood beside Ella and squeezed her hand tight. The reddish light shone like a lantern, cutting through the mist of the dark graveyard, permeating everything. The music stuttered to a stop and gasps trickled through the crowd of ghosts, who were turning to stare. They may as well not have existed at all.

"I love you, Ella."

Able stepped forward then, his face awash in consternation., "I want nothing but happiness for y'both, but you don't know what this can lead to. It's not that I mind the rules, I'm known to bend 'em this way an' that, but some of 'em y'can't break. Some things that break can't be fixed. We can't be having anything like that happening to our Ella…can we Thomas?"

"I know, I know." Thomas yelled. He dropped her hand, pacing and looking around as if there was a solution lying on the ground somewhere. His blue hue had returned to its more common green, but this green was too bright, too hot, edged in red. He stopped, looking weary and defeated.

"I can't let anything happen to her. She is the only thing that matters to me now. You and Elizabeth can't be harmed either— Ella would never forgive me."

Thomas turned to Ella, tears of green streaking down his angelic blue face. "Ella, if we cannot have our happiness, we can at least have a memory of what it might have been."

The more he spoke, the deeper she sank into despair and certainty. In her heart, all she wanted was him, at any cost. In her mind, she loved Able and Elizabeth and would never jeopardize them. She watched his face, looking for some glimmer of hope, and missed his meaning. *What moment?* At the risk of embarrassing herself and ruining the magic, she had to ask.

"What moment, Thomas?"

"This one."

He pulled her tight against him, cold and sparkling and electric, and kissed her with every ounce of his being. Bright pink light cascaded from the top of his head and scanned down slowly as the kiss continued. She could feel it spreading into her chest, her lungs, her mind, her heart—there was no escaping the cold heat of Thomas' kiss. The connection, the electricity between them consumed all there was, leaving them in a bubble of passion. At that moment, she was not in a cemetery, she wasn't even on earth; she was in heaven and there was nothing else.

Unbeknownst to her, several other things had happened in the same moment.

Beyond the gate, Sara and Nancy had parked the dusty old truck and were making their way to the cemetery.

Able, too far away to separate the lovers in time, tried to tackle Thomas and instead passed right through him.

Elizabeth stood, her face a rictus scream, full of pain and terror and loss.

"ELLA NO!!"

Able and Elizabeth's cries slowly brought Ella back down to reality, as more sounds of panic resonated through the crowd. But before she could pull away from the kiss, she felt a jolt of electricity unlike anything before. This wasn't the electricity of a kiss, or of a spirit's touch—it *hurt*, sending a wave of pain through her whole body. She doubled over, reaching out toward Able and Elizabeth as the pain shot through her again.

"Ella! Ella!"

In the distance, she could hear two voices that didn't belong—Nancy and Sara were here! The pain knocked her to her knees, and she realized that she couldn't catch her breath, couldn't even whisper out a warning to the Jamboree to disappear. Thomas, panicking, tried to lift her up to standing in his arms...and it worked.

As the last wave of pain subsided, realization took its place.

She was no longer standing in the decrepit graveyard. It was still Harrington, only it was a dazzling spectacle, well maintained with nothing old, tattered or broken. Elevated tombstones were draped in lush, rich fabrics—velvet and brocade—embellished with ornate gold trim and intricate patterns that shouted their opulence. Bright, jewel-toned banners fluttered from the towering obeli and mausoleums, their silks and satins catching the light as they rippled in the gentle breeze. Every corner of the cemetery was alive with color and movement—vivid floral arrangements in towering vases, massive candelabras illuminating peach faces, and shimmering ribbons woven into the décor. A sea of fresh magnolia blossoms created an intoxicating blend of wealth and southern charm, while a crystal white moon cast a warm, sparkling glow over the bright and vivid spirits…no, people!

For there they were, dressed in their bright and funereal best, as solid and real as the very stones where they stood. The only thing that hadn't changed was a pale tint of blue that limned their bodies, but in every other respect they were as alive as-

As alive as I am.

In front of her stood the soldier she loved, in full flesh and blood. She would never have guessed that he would have such captivating sea-green eyes. Still dressed in Mr. Weatherton's tux, the suit was no longer tattered. Instead, it looked like it was just made yesterday, shiny lapels impeccably stitched. It was like watching *The Wizard of Oz* for the first time and seeing him in full color almost burst her heart with excitement.

"Are you… are you alive?"

The excitement was not mirrored in Thomas, his face a mask of dread.

"No, Ella! You are in the realm of the dead! Look." Thomas pointed, directing her to turn around.

She turned to stare straight into her own face. It was slack and catatonic, tilted upward as though awaiting a kiss from the moon. Her skin had turned the same glowing blue as the spirits had been, but there were no flames in her eyes—instead they were white as the marble headstones, and as bereft of life.

I am not in my body.

Panic crept in as she turned to look at Able and Elizabeth.

Elizabeth, tears running down her cheeks, buried her face in Able's shoulder.

"ELLA!"

Sara and Nancy were closing in on the gate.

Then there was fire.

Even in this world, Annalee chose to wear her flames. They licked, red and hungry around her body, and in a few places, Ella could see where the skin was bubbling. She trembled, and Thomas' embrace could do nothing to stop the fear.

"We have to leave," ordered Annalee. "Now. There's nothing we can do for Ella here in this moment—we have to disappear before her friends see us as well. This is a desperate enough breach of our laws; heaven forfend that the girl breaks more rules and bring a more dire fate upon herself. Begone! Quickly!"

The four of them turned to the burning woman, who gathered them up to her like children frightened of a storm.

"Come now, all of you. We must away."

"But Ella…"

Annalee hushed Thomas with a raised finger "… Is as good as dead for the moment. We can't help her if we're caught."

Able shook his head. "A body can't live without its spirit; we can't leave here!"

"Would you risk her damnation for all eternity over such a little thing as a body?"

Reluctantly, they started to move away from the cemetery gates.

"Wait!" cried Ella. "What are we doing? I can't leave, that's my body, we can't—"

"Do you want your friends to end up like you?"

She could hear them bickering their way down the path. Nancy and Sara, her best friends. The best friends she had ignored in favor of this one night each year. Her real friends.

"N-no."

"Then move."

It cost her. Each step away from her body felt like stepping further and further into the heart of an iceberg. The cold was starting to bite and score and tear at her mind. Thomas and Able wrapped their arms around her as her steps started to falter, and Elizabeth wrapped a cape around her as she shivered. She didn't know where their steps were taking them, just that she was moving *away*, and that she might never come back.

Elizabeth was crying, softly glowing blue tears on a pale pearly face.

"Oh Able." she whispered. "Not again."

#   #   #

"ELLA!"

Nancy shook her for what had to have been the hundredth time. Sara had already thrown up twice. No matter what they said, what they did (Sara had tried slapping her across the face, with the argument that it worked in the movies,) Ella would not snap out of it. She simply sat on the grass, eyes open, breath shallow, staring empty-eyed at the moon.

That was the worst part. *Where were her eyes?*

Sara couldn't take it. Snatching up a flashlight, she started marching back to the entrance.

"Where are you going?!"

"T' get somethin'!" she bellowed back.

Nancy shook Ella again. Nothing. Not even a change in her breathing. It was like looking at someone on life support but without all the hoses and weird beeping machines. The lights were on—but there was nobody home.

"What do we do, what do we do, oh God what do we *do?*"

A heavy backpack thudded to the ground at her feet. It was Ella's.

"We read," said Sara firmly, starting to pull out the notebooks and spreading them in the grass.

"If there's an answer, it's in here somewhere."
Slowly and grimly, Nancy nodded. Together they sat next to the cold, empty body of their friend—and read ghost stories.

MR. RON

BY JOSH SPERO

Introducing Mr. Ron

Who could not keep his flesh on.

His skin would sag and turn to gray,

Tape, glue, or staples; it would not stay.

His skin was changing slow and steady,

(he did not know he'd died already.)

Eventually he began to smell,

And then his body started to swell.

The worse he got, the more he grew shy,

And ironically thought, *I wish I'd just die.*

He became a recluse and never was seen,

Because he felt that he looked so obscene.

But then he had a sweet realization,

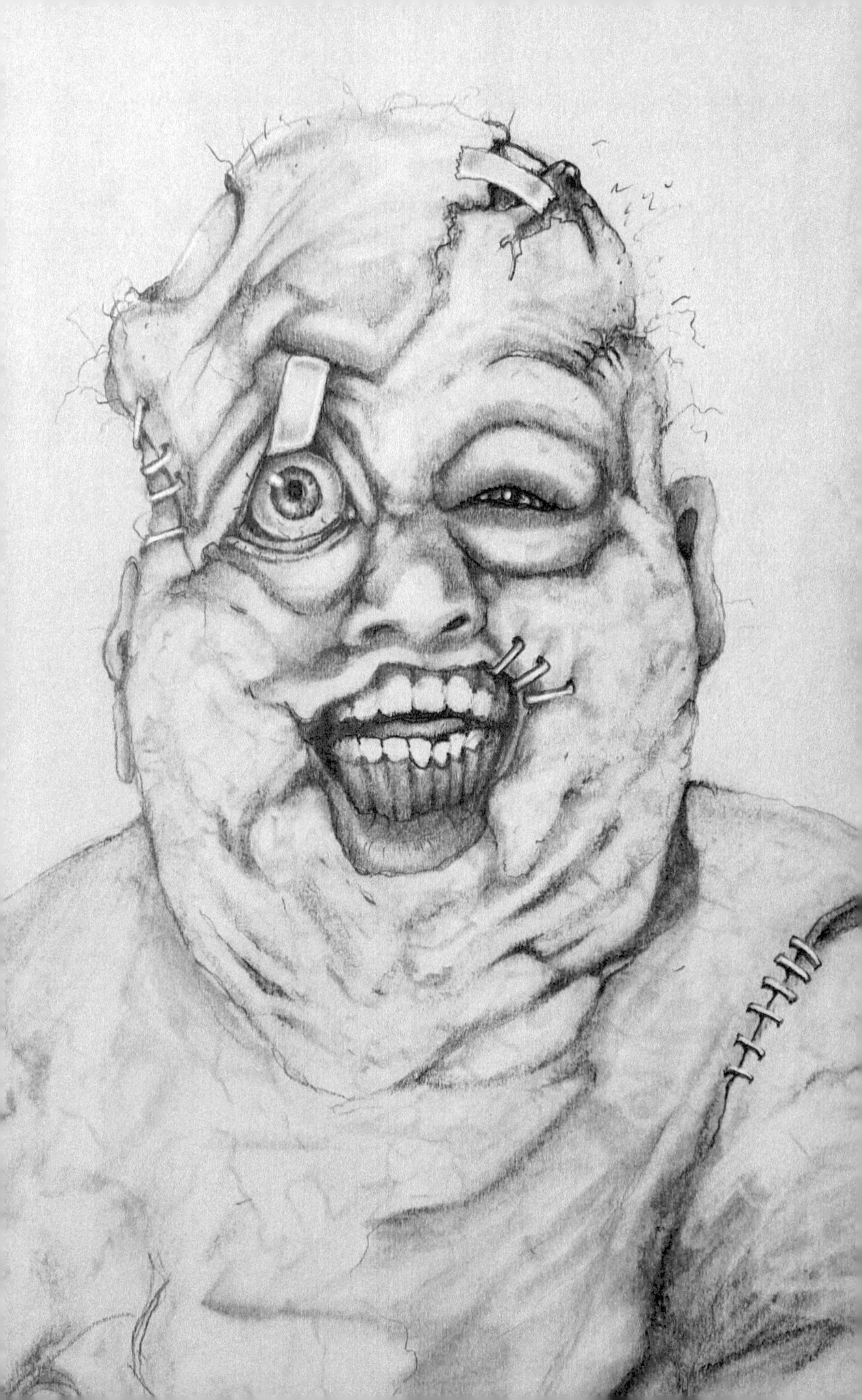

There *was* one day he might not cause a sensation—

He realized, "Next week will be Halloween!"

He could walk through the streets without a big scene.

So, that's what he did and had a great time,

Even though he was covered in grime.

All through the year he lives alone,

But on All Hollows Eve, with the midnight bell tone,

He comes out of hiding to see all the sights,

So look out for him on Halloween nights.

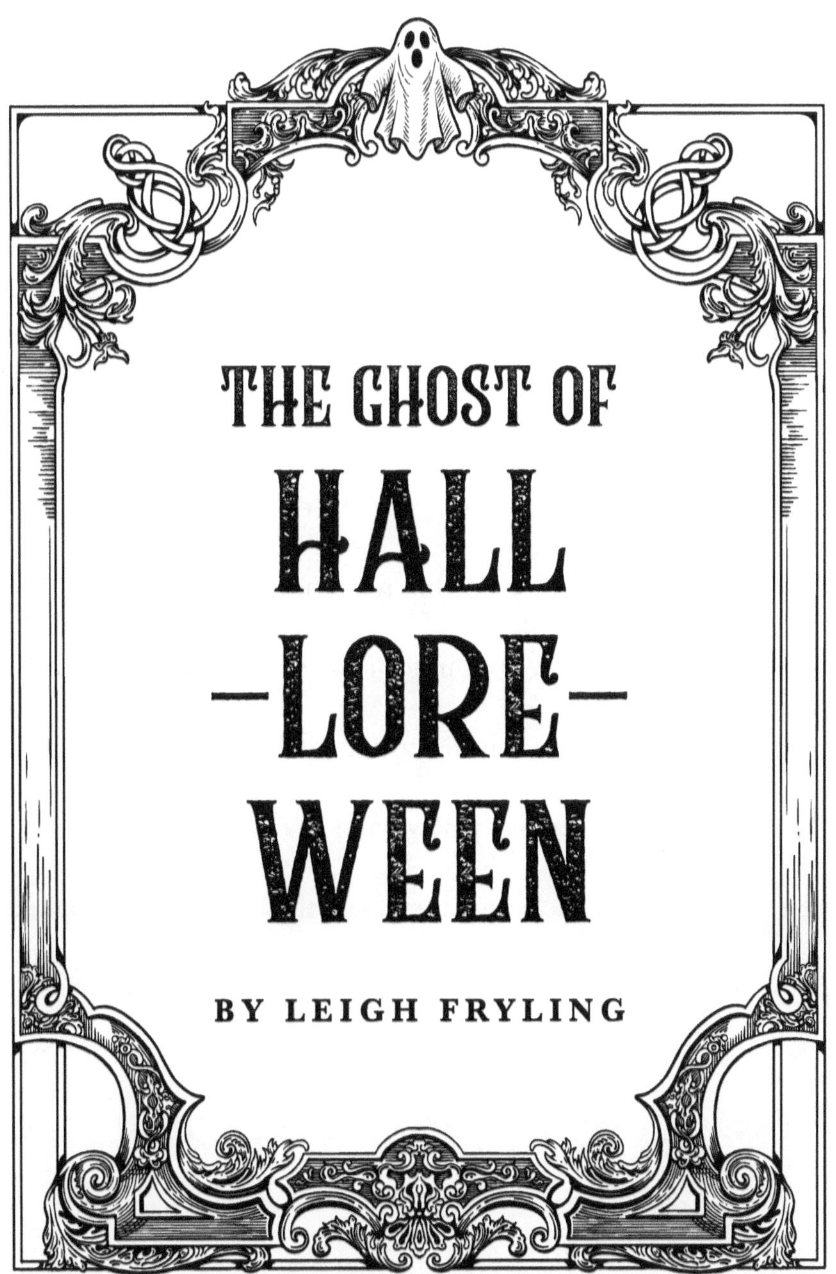
THE GHOST OF
HALL
-LORE-
WEEN
BY LEIGH FRYLING

1	2	3	4	5	6	7	8	9	10	11	12	13	14	15
32	3	1	10	2	29	22	7	29	7	14	8	19	22	9

1 There is a ghost within this book, she floats between the lines-

2 She haunts the pages one by one and shivers up the spine.

3 If you ask her whether anyone has read these tomes before,

4 She'll only grin and wave you in the cracked and creaking door.

5 She disappears between your fears, her laughter soft and hollow,

6 Where'ere she goes, the story flows, and you are bound to follow.

7 You'd almost swear she wasn't there, and then you hear her sighing,

8 Between the screams and bitter dreams, the living and the dying.

9 Her shadow cast, she walks the last few moments of a story,

10 Then turns away, as though to say, '*Well, wasn't that one gory!*'

11 The tale is told, your blood runs cold, she beckons toward another-

12 Her ghoulish fun is never done, until you close the cover.

13 She leaves her mark twixt light and dark, a poem, a verse, a legend,

14 Her trail is here, but still unclear, is where her name gets mentioned.

15 There is a ghost within this book, she walks these tales unseen—

16 But never fear, she's always near, the Ghost of Hall-Lore-Ween!

Please forgive me; you caught me during
one of my favorite activities: making
a man-o'-lantern. It's just mindless
entertainment. This next story is one of
my favorites. Here's the scoop.

Jacko

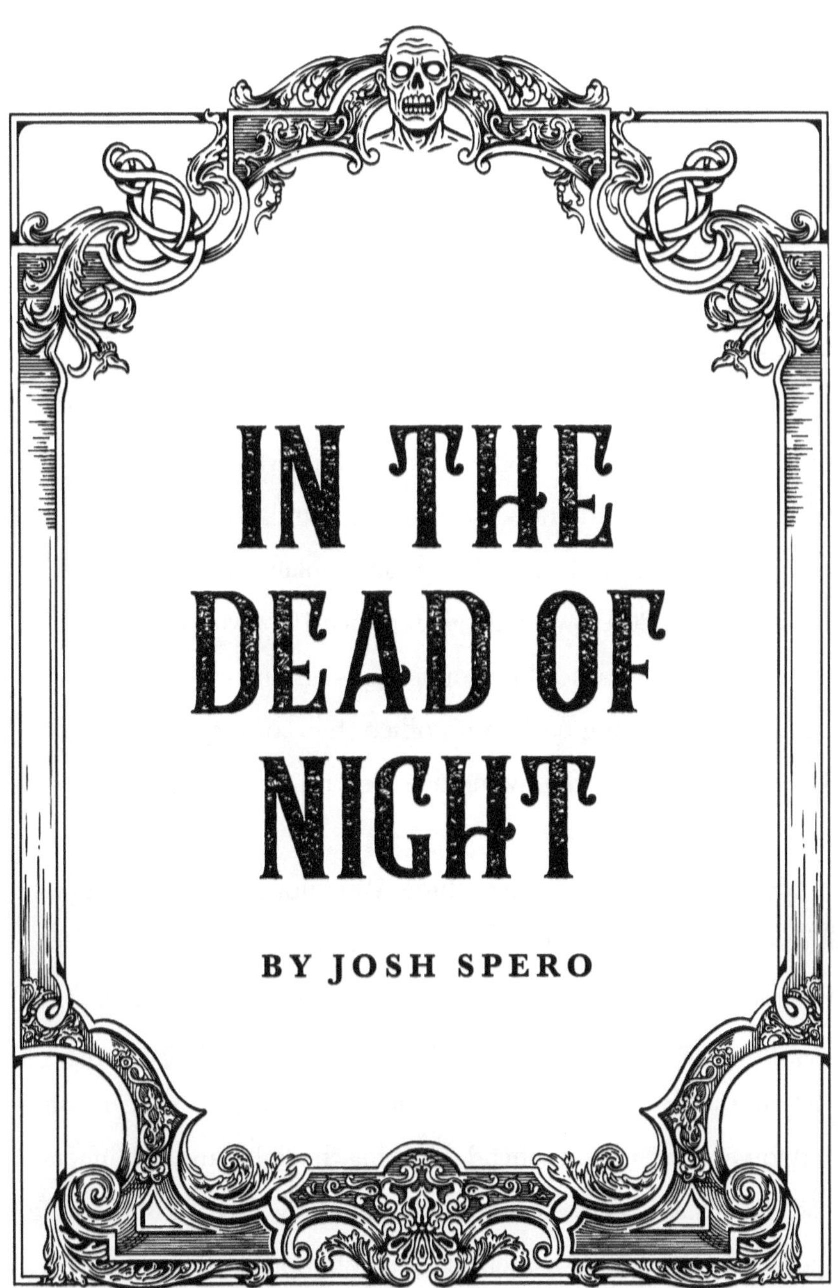

IN THE DEAD OF NIGHT

BY JOSH SPERO

November 2, Sunday night, 7:00 pm

It was a quiet and dreary Sunday night at the Maryville, Colorado police station. Nothing had happened for weeks, and nothing was happening now. In cop talk, Sunday nights were dead. A perfect night to schedule a lone rookie cop to look after the whopping 3,200 townsfolk, give or take 10% who were out of town for The Big Game. The young cop, legs crossed with feet up on his desk, was reclining back in his office chair and trying not to be jealous of the various family members currently attending The Big Game.

He sighed. Back to the nothing. Well, not entirely nothing—he still had a stack of paperwork to fill out about last night's escapades. But it would be hard for anyone to blame him for avoiding the cold, sterile forms lying on the corner of the desk; no one wants to fill out the details of a friend's accidental death. His officer's hat tilted forward over his forehead, blocking the light, and his fingers laced comfortably across his midsection as he waited for something, anything, to happen. If something didn't happen soon, he really would have to start on Lucas's death paperwork. He nearly fell out of his chair when the office phone, ringing like the bells of glory, freed him from his slumberous break.

"Officer Steven Beckley, at your service. How may I assist you?" the young man declared. The voice on the other line was fast and incoherent. "Hold on, Jimmy! I cannot understand a word you are saying. A little slower now. What happened?"

Jimmy Rowe was the town's mortician and the one in charge of all the locally deceased, which was impressive given his age. Most people weren't comfortable turning their loved ones over to a grinning 24-year-old, but Jimmy was nothing if not relatively professional. Most of the time. He had not been available last night to process Lucas's body (for reasons that were not entirely professional) and was making up for lost time this evening. At least, that's what he was supposed to be doing.

"The dead are waking up, man! This is far out! I mean total zombie apocalypse! You know how they found Lucas dead yesterday? Well, he isn't dead anymore. He's a total freaking zombie, man. He just tried to attack me and everything!"

"Jimmy, you need to stop watching those horror movies. This is the third call this month about some kind of strange phenomenon."

"No, man! I'm telling you! This is real. Get all the gun power you can. Doomsday is here, man! I'm talking bring grenades, a rocket launcher, the whole nine, man—" Jimmy cried, a genuine note of panic in his voice. Steve frowned into the phone.

"Alright, Jimmy. I'll head over there to check it out after I finish all my reports."

Before Jimmy could retort, Steven hung up the phone, kicked

his feet back up and re-tilted his hat. About fifteen minutes later, another call came in. This time it was from Mrs. Tully; an older widow recluse that spent her days staring at the world through the slightly open slats of her front window blinds.

"Mrs. Tully?"

A shrill, also panicking voice ripped through the phone cord and into his eardrum. Steve held the phone away from his ear.

"Mrs. Tully, now wait just a… A zombie? Come on now, Mrs. Tully, did Jimmy put you up to this?"

More brain breaking noises came from the receiver.

"Jimmy Rowe, the mortician, he-—MRS. TULLY!"

He was starting to get angry.

"This isn't funny, you know. You are both clogging up the line in case a real emergency comes in. Please respect the law and knock this off, okay? Please tell Jimmy to knock it off as well, and that he is not going to get one over on me."

He slammed down the receiver, then stared at the phone, daring it to ring. A minute passed. Two. Blissful, if uneasy, silence. He turned and started to walk the 15 steps to the coffee machine.

RINGA RINGA RING RING.

Steve groaned to himself, turned, and with a resigned sigh picked up the phone.

He wouldn't put it down again for another ½ hour.

"Steven, it's Mary Bird, there's a-—"

"Officer, you won't believe me, but there's a -—"

"Please, you have to help me, I just saw a -—"

Zombie.

Zombie.

Zombie.

The clincher was when Reverend Abrams called. Reverend Abrams was so stern that he wouldn't lie even if it would save his life.

"Lucas Melbourne has arisen from the dead and is running toward the centre of town; I can see him from the vestry window. Which is very inconvenient because his funeral is scheduled for Wednesday. I suggest that he be returned to a corpse state post haste."

"Reverend Abrams, I—"

"Son, stop talking to me and call for backup. Then get someone, *anyone*, out here with a gun. Preferably several someones and several guns."

There was a click, and the line went dead. Without further ado, he hung up, then started dialing. Cantreville sheriff's office; no answer. Meldon sheriff's office; no answer. Vickersberg; no answer.

It's just me. I'm all that's left.

Steve glanced around the office, and his eyes fell on the arms locker.

Time to Rambo up.

He was just buckling on the last clip of ammo when the phone rang once more. He took a deep breath, thought about ignoring it, and then answered it anyway.

"Officer Steven Beckley, yes I believe you there are zombies, who is this and what is your situation?"

"Lucas just broke into my house, zombie Lucas. Please help! We are being attacked!"

The call came from Michael Maber, the local computer tech guy and videogame-oholic. Steve was honestly a little annoyed. If anyone besides Jimmy in this town had a zombie plan, it would be Mike. Luckily for Mike, his was also the house nearest to the station out of all the evening's calls.

"I'm on my way Mike. Is Sandy with you?"

"Yeah, but she passed out. She freaked and fainted. Maybe send the paramedics too?" he sobbed.

"Where in the house are you? Are you safe at the moment?"

"We made it to my game room, and we are locked inside."

"Okay! Please barricade yourself in. I'll be right there! Just stay alive!"

"He's trying to break the door down. Hurry!" yelled Mike.

Steve didn't bother putting the phone back in its cradle. There would be no more desk duty tonight.

The entire ride to Mike's, he scanned the streets for zombies. The moon was high and bright making the streets easy to view. Instead, all that he saw were multiple people packing their cars frantically, as if to flee for their lives. It was chaos through the residential streets. A panic set into this town and Steven was praying for the strength to face the zombies alone. He tried his service cell, the CB radio, hell he tried messaging other officers on their socials… nothing but dead silence.

In the bright moonlight it was easy to see Sandy spilling out of the front window, scared and stumbling as the cruiser came to a stop. Mike dove out of the window right after her, running smack into Sandy on the landing and knocking them both to the ground. Then

he saw Lucas.

Reaching out of the window after them was barely recognizable as human, let alone as their friend Lucas. The creature's eyes were a milky white, with a spattering of black as though the pupil had shattered across the surface of the eye into dozens of gaping slits. Where his bangs had been *those stupid 90's bowl cut bangs he had been so proud of* the white glare of bone shards protruded, the skull exploding outward from beneath the forehead, smeared with gobs of dried and drying…something. Something dark and wet and sticky looking. The flesh from its right cheek was missing, revealing the broken teeth underneath. The stench of old blood and rot permeated from the living corpse that he could smell from forty feet away.

Mike and Sandy stood, frozen like deer in headlights when the police car came screeching to a halt. They didn't even notice that the zombie had slipped out of the window behind them.

"Police! Freeze or I'll shoot! Not you Mike you idiot, RUN!"

The zombie that had been Lucas stopped for a second and then redirected its attention to Steve. It raised its arms towards him. It groaned a throaty groan and took one step forward.

BANG

His gun went off and the zombie dropped to the ground like a sack of potatoes. It was the first time Steve had ever fired his gun. It was not going to be the last.

Earlier…

Michael Maber was returning home from an impromptu

memorial service for his long-time best friend Lucas Melbourne. Memorial service was a stretch, it was more like a bunch of friends sitting around a campfire, telling stories, and drowning their sorrow as they mourned. But not Mike. Instead, he drove home sober, shooting disappointed glances towards his nearly blacked out girlfriend Sandy Galloway. She drank so much, so fast, that he had no choice but to be the designated driver.

Home, Mike helped Sandy stumble up the front steps and through the front door. They managed to stagger down the entry hall and into the living room before Sandy lost her balance, and rolled backwards over the arm of the couch, legs pointing straight up at the ceiling, giggling the whole way.

Watching the whole thing, Mike let go of his resentment and laughed. "I always knew you were head over heels for me, babe." He giggled. "Stay put. I'll be back; I've got to pee." He turned and shuffled down another hall to the nearest bathroom.

Sandy did as she was told and stayed there. It wasn't too long before quaint little snores resonated through the quiet house.

She awoke to the feeling of Mike's hand on her right ankle. Another giggle broke out. "Help me up, Mike. I've fallen and I can't get up," she mumbled sleepily.

The hand tightened. Something was wrong. She sat bolt upright—the hand on her ankle was rough and coarse, not like Mike's at all. Panic set in as she rubbed her eyes, trying to get a look at who was grabbing her.

A rotting corpse, eyes white, blood running from its mouth and forehead, struggled to its feet in front of her. Sandy belted a bloodcurdling scream as she started flailing, kicking her feet like she was pedaling a bicycle. She managed to kick the creature square in the jaw causing it to lose its balance. Just as it stumbled backwards, a vase flew in from the other side of the room, just barely missing its head and shattering on the floor.

The commotion caused the zombie to lose its balance as it crashed through an end table and onto the floor.

"Sandy, RUN!"

She did not run. Her eyes rolled to the back of her skull, and she started to go down faster than Mike could cover the distance. He ran, tripped, and stumbled across the room, catching her just in time and throwing her over his shoulder in a fireman's carry. He lurched to his game room, knocking over knick knacks and books before he made it to the door which he shut and locked behind him. He placed Sandy in the loveseat and conducted a very quick body search, looking for any bite marks she may have received. Her skin was completely intact. *Oh, thank God. What the hell is going on? That looked just like Lucas*, Mike thought to himself as he frantically called 911.

Someone picked up. "Officer Steven Beckley, at your service. How may I assist you?"

"Steve, a zombie just broke into my house, and it looks like Lucas. Please help! We are being attacked!" Halfway through the call, the zombie started banging on the door as if to beat it down.

"He's trying to break the door down. Hurry!" Mike screamed as his phone went dead. "Damn it!" Mike threw his phone aside. "Stupid battery!"

"What happened? Where did..." Sandy was coming to but was

still in a state of panic.

"Hey babe. You're okay. We're okay at the moment, but…" *BAM!* The door slammed again, this time starting a crack in the center of it. Startled, Sandy started crying hysterically. Mike's eyes quickly bounced around the room, like a ping pong ball in a small wooden box. "There!" Mike said, pointing at the window. "We'll go out the window and run for safety."

"What if there are more out there?" Sandy wailed. Just then the door broke a little more exposing the face of the zombie on the other side. All inhibition quite literally flew out of the window as they both sprang to their feet. Mike threw open the window. "GO! NOW! I'm right behind you!"

She clambered out as the door finally broke completely and the zombie plowed through. Mike could feel the swinging of its arms right behind him as he dove out the window behind Sandy. As he hit the ground, the lights and sirens of a cop car came to a screeching halt, leaving tire tracks in his driveway. They were so happy to see Steven that they hardly noticed the zombie had slipped out of the window behind them.

The zombie rose to its feet and began stumbling toward Mike and Sandy. "Police! Freeze or I'll shoot! Not you Mike you idiot, RUN!"

The zombie stopped for a second, then redirected its attention to the officer. It raised its arms towards him. It groaned a throaty groan and took one step towards him.

BANG

His gun went off and the zombie was flung to the ground like a sack of potatoes.

Earlier…

Lucas woke up in a very dark place. He figured that it must be the middle of the night, based on the darkness. Yet he did not see the usual glow of his little plastic jack-o-lantern night light. He tried to sit up but bumped his head on something hard before he could even make it up onto his elbows. He raised his hand to try and feel out what he had hit, and his hand touched cold metal three inches above his head. Even more confused, he tried to slide out of his bed sideways but was yet again stopped by something cold and hard. He started feeling the space around him and quickly realized he was enclosed in some sort of box.

Panic set in and fear overtook him. He tried to scream, but all that came out was a breathy groan. His throat ached. He started hitting and pounding on the walls around him, but the walls were too thick and hard. After a while, Lucas calmed himself down and tried to think back to the last thing he could remember. Absolutely nothing came to mind, which set him off into another panic-stricken thrashing about.

Shortly into this second flailing, he heard a rapping on the wall behind his head. "Hello!" a voice cried out. Lucas tried to respond, yet only another grunt escaped his lips. The sounds of metal screeching echoed throughout the box like a blanket of sound. Suddenly, a thin line of light crept in through the top of the box. The surface he was lying on began to move. As he slid backwards, the light became brighter and brighter, blinding him before the floor beneath him stopped moving. He groaned and tried to reach up to cover his burning eyes.

"Oh my God! You're alive!" a blur that he thought might be a man wearing a white lab coat shouted.

Lucas sat up and looked around, struggling to see past the black spots that rolled across his vision. Metal slab, lab equipment, lockers…the morgue! He was in the freaking morgue! He turned to the lab technician and reached out for help.

"Z…Z…ZOMBIE! AHHHHHH!" the man screamed while throwing his clipboard into the air behind him, as he ran out of the door in haste.

Zombie? Lucas thought to himself. *Why would he say that? What is wrong with me?*

He tried to walk, but his feet were not cooperating with the directions that his brain was sending. He stumbled over to a mirror above a sink in the corner of the room. His face was covered in dry blood from a gash in his forehead. His eyes had turned bleach white. He had a section of flesh on his right cheek missing, with muscle tissue and broken teeth exposed underneath. There was what looked like teeth marks on his neck, also with some skin missing, and his teeth were stained crimson. Even with blurry vision, he looked at himself and thought, *Holy shit, I'm a zombie!*

Far out, he thought. *How did I get like this? Where am I? How am I going to get home? Where is home from here?*

The graveness of the situation dawned and all he could think was, *I need to get out of here before that man comes back with the cavalry.* He had seen the ending of *The Night of the Living Dead* and wanted no part of it. Luckily, the building that he was in was only one story, and he was able to stumble out the back door without being discovered. Before he left, he saw a sign in the building that said **Thank You for Visiting Hanniger Hospital**. *This is good*, he thought. *I know this hospital. It's not that far.*

Under a deep autumn nightfall, he started to stagger down the street, committed to making the long trek on foot.

Okay, what do we know about zombies? Horribly mangled but still moving? Check. Moans and Groans? Check. Insatiable hunger for human flesh? Just then his stomach responded with a loud audible grumble. *I guess check.*

His thoughts were broken abruptly by the sound of someone screaming nearby. The round and familiar form of Mrs. Tully had been getting something out of the trunk of her car in her driveway. She must have seen him and panicked; she ran inside her house and slammed her door. Then he saw her peaking through her blinds with a phone held up to ear.

That's not good, he thought to himself as he ambled off. *Okay*, he thought, *obviously, I need to get off of the streets. Where can I go? I live too far to walk home like this, and there's no Uber driver on God's green earth that would pick me up… Michael lives just past the Church. That's six blocks from here. He's my ride-or-die. He'll understand. I hope…*

He stumbled the six blocks trying his best not to be seen but failing miserably. Reverend Abrams was out front locking the doors after evening bible study, when he witnessed Lucas staggering by. The Reverend's eyes grew wide as he started spouting the Lord's Prayer and making the sign of the cross.

Lucas tried to say, "I'm sorry," but all that came out was

"mmmhhhuuuu". The Reverend slammed the heavy wooden door, and Lucas could hear the bolt slide home. So much for help from that quarter.

Finally, he rounded the corner of the street where Michael lived. Taking one uncoordinated step after another, he eventually made it to the front door only to discover that it was locked. Instead of pounding on it and making a scene, Lucas figured he'd mosey into the back yard; Michael never locked his sliding glass door. He'd always claimed it would make for an easier exit in case of a fire or a zombie apocalypse. *Joke's on him.*

Lucas was very pleased to be correct. The back door slid open, and he shuffled inside. The sliding door led to the living room where he saw Sandy lying backwards over the armrest of Mike's sofa and snoring ever so gently. He stared at her for a moment in an attempt to figure out why her feet were sticking straight up towards the ceiling. He grabbed her ankle in an effort to wake her up.

She started to stir as he heard her start to giggle. He heard her say, "Help me up, Mike. I've fallen and I can't get up." After an awkward moment of silence, she looked up to see him. A look of absolute terror set into her face as she screamed and started flailing, kicking frantically. She managed to kick Lucas square in the jaw causing him to lose his balance. Just as he stumbled backwards, a vase flew in from the side just missing his nose by a millimeter. He started stumbling back further, tripping over a little end table and crashing through it.

Mike cried out, "Sandy, RUN!" But the sight of Lucas had sent Sandy's consciousness packing, forcing Mike to scoop a limp Sandy over his shoulder and run them both into the safety of the game room. He slammed and locked the door.

Panic set into Lucas. *Holy Crap,* he thought to himself. *This is so bad; so very bad. I need to let them know that I'm not here to eat them. I just need them to understand. I need help.* He started down the hall to the game room door. *I need to get in. If they call the cops or the military or something, I'm so screwed.* Lucas placed his ear on the door to see what they were doing in there. He heard Michael on the phone.

"Noooooo" he tried to say only it just came out "mmmhhhuuu". He proceeded to bang on the door. This phone call ended, but the more time that passed since the phone call, the more desperate he became. He started to pound on that door harder and harder until he eventually punched a huge hole right in the center of it. *Damn it. I'll buy him a new door. I can't stop now.* He looked through the hole to see Michael lifting up the window for Sandy to jump through. Lucas reached through the hole in the door and unlocked it from the inside. Fully bought in, Lucas went headfirst out of that same window just one second behind Michael and landed on the ground with a hard thud.

Just as he hit that ground, his vision went white. At first, he assumed that it was from the fall, but then he realized that there were headlights and a bright spotlight on him. Before Lucas could get his bearings about him, he staggered to his feet and heard, "Police! Freeze or I'll shoot! Not you Mike you idiot, RUN!"

Wait a second. I know that voice. It's Steven Beckley. I went to school with his older brother Evan Beckley. Yeah. Steven used to try to hang out with us. We'd tell him to get friends his own age and put him in headlocks.

Lucas stood and reached out to the officer. "Steven. Don't Shoot. It's me, Lucas."

BANG

An intense and sharp pain shot through his left shoulder, sending him tumbling. In shock and disbelief, Lucas cried out, "OOOOOOUCH! What the hell?"

He sat up and looked around. Everyone was frozen in an expression of dumbfounded awe. For a very brief instant the surprise almost masked the pain in his shoulder before it came flooding back.

"Oh my goodness, guys. I'm really hurt." Lucas said as he laid back down holding his gunshot wound. Suddenly, his vision and consciousness went black.

Much later…

Lucas woke up in a hospital room to the sound of rhythmic beeping. Completely confused he looked around this new room and saw both Mike and Sandy sitting near his bedside.

"Hey, Lucas. How are you feel, buddy?" Mike asked, his voice a mix of anxiety and wonder.

"Where am I? What happened?" Lucas asked in a hoarse whisper.

"Ah man. Do I have a story to tell you." Mike replied. "So, do you remember the Halloween party that you went to on Friday? Remember Sandy wouldn't let me go because my ex was supposed to be there?"

"Um… Yeah. That's the last thing I remember. Why?" Lucas

chimed in.

"Well, apparently you got really drunk there, and then decided to drive yourself home. You fell asleep behind the wheel on your way home that night. You drove off the ravine overpass bridge by the old 31 highway and knocked your noggin. You were in a coma. Luckily, they found you when they did."

Lucas shook his head gingerly as though to clear it while Mike continued. "The only thing is, apparently you dressed up like a very realistic zombie that night. They found you the next day, but Old Doc Miller took one look at you and declared you dead, dude. I mean he's so old he doesn't even know what century he's in."

Mike raised his eyebrows and curved the right corner of his lips. "Well, the good news is you weren't dead. I guess you woke up in the morgue, scared the shit out of Jimmy Rowe, and you started walking around the streets freaking out all the townsfolk. These doctors said you were dealing with short term memory loss, severe dehydration...basically your systems were pretty much offline. Plus when you crashed you gashed your forehead pretty good. You got some stitches there, but they say you'll have a cool-looking scar. Oh, and the exposed cheek and broken teeth? Just prosthetics dude. Nice touch. So yeah! Welcome back! I'm glad you're alive, man. We were all so devastated." Mike clapped a hand on Lucas's good shoulder, laughing as Lucas winced. Sandy didn't look quite as enthusiastic, but she also muttered something about being glad he was alive.

"You guys have a funny way of showing it. Please thank Steven for me for being a terrible shot." Lucas said while trying to adjust his sling. "What does a guy got to do to get some food around here? I'm so hungry I could eat the next person who gets in range!"

The room grew silent as the atmosphere changed from camaraderie to concern. Mike and Sandy exchange a worried glance.

"What, too soon?" Lucas chuckled.

Mike let out the air in his lungs and smirked. "Come on, bud. You're not a zombie anymore. I'll get a nurse to bring you some real food. Humans are off the menu, dude!"

Now I lay me down to dream,

This Hall-Lore-Ween has been a scream.

Monsters, zombies, ghosts galore

Gasps and giggles by the score.

The fiends and I now take our rest

But next year's haunts will bring our best.

Book Three awaits with tricks in store,

More ghoulish fun and ghastly lore.

My frightful friend, just wait and see,

'Til then be safe and stay spooky.

Look at me. I'm a regular

Dead-gar Allen Poe! 'Til next time.

Jacko

ABOUT THE AUTHOR

Growing up, **Josh Spero** was always fascinated with Halloween and the darker side of things. As a child, he looked forward to the spooky season all year, eagerly awaiting his chance to visit the pumpkin patch, decorate the house with cobwebs and pumpkins, and immerse himself in horror movies and ghost stories. As he grew, his love for all things horror and macabre intensified. His affinity for the season soon became a lifestyle, inspiring him to write and create these spooky tales.

He obtained a Bachelor's Degree in Kinesiology: Exercise Science and a Master's in Applied Exercise Science. Armed with knowledge and imagination, he created this world of twisted tales to entertain and thrill readers of all ages. Through his stories, Josh hopes to capture the spirit of Halloween and inspire others to embrace their love for all things spooky. He lives in Los Angeles with his wife, Robin, and their dog Bailee. He remains enthusiastic about the holiday and is eager to share his spooky tales with others!

SPECIAL GUEST AUTHOR

Leigh Fryling has been correcting everyone's grammar since the 4th grade. In 5th grade she was nicknamed 'The Dictionary', as in 'go ask The Dictionary'. This moniker was particularly onerous when it came to group projects. From there it was a slippery downhill slope from being an annoying know-it-all to an itinerant freelance editor, ghost writer, and high school teacher. She specializes in inventing new classes and curriculum, running the Drama Club, and is careening her way through motherhood with all the grace of a newborn giraffe attempting algebra. None of this would be possible without the steady and unwavering support of her heroically stoic husband Zach, the bemused backing of her family and friends, and the oblivious proximity of the family cats who view the editing process as prime lap time. When she isn't listening to horror podcasts while washing the dishes, she can be found building her cozy Hobbit lifestyle, playing in a folk band, and crafting with friends.

INTERIOR ARTIST

TT Hernandez is a multidisciplinary artist, fascinated by the human experience. She has captured the visual narrative for award winning poets, international journalists, lauded composers, and New York Times bestselling authors. Her artwork has been featured internationally at Sundance Film Festival, PBS's POV Docs, Prague & Nottingham International Film Festivals, France Télévisons, One World Media Awards, International Documentary Festival in France, The Boston Globe, M.I.T Museum, The Irish Consulate Boston, and more.

COVER ARTIST

My name is **Aldo Avelar.** As an illustrator I have a passion for art, imagery, and drawing that has shaped my journey. Graduating from California State University of Long Beach in the class of 2020, I began my artistic pursuits during my second year of college. Although I started later than my peers, my love for art drove me to catch up and surpass expectations. Devoting an entire year to drawing every day, both in and out of class, I honed my skills and emerged as one of the top students in my graduating class. Inspirations from legendary artists such as Albrecht Dürer, Michelangelo, and James Jean have motivated me to continually strive for higher standards. While my artistic journey is still ongoing, I remain dedicated to working hard and pushing boundaries to achieve even greater heights.

If you enjoyed *It's Hall-Lore-Ween Again* try the first book in the series: *Hall-Lore-Ween*! Or check out these great spookie stories!

MONSTER KID DETECTIVE SQUAD

Book 1: Elsie Frankenstein and the Case of the Disappearing Dogs

Book 2: Sherry Dracula and the Case of the Lunchroom Phantom

Book 3: Rico Gillman and the Case of the See-Through Woman

Find us on amazon.com

castlebridgemedia.com

or ask for us in your favorite bookstore.

(Thank you for your reviews!)